I SEE YOU

Elle Gray

Copyright © 2020 by Elle Gray

All rights reserved.

No part of this book may be reproduced in any form or by any electronic or mechanical means, including information storage and retrieval systems, without written permission from the author, except for the use of brief quotations in a book review.

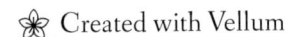

❀ Created with Vellum

PROLOGUE
PAXTON

Seattle Police HQ; Downtown Seattle

"Over your nine years with Seattle PD, you have put together quite a record, Detective Arrington."

"I was always told that when I put my mind to something, I tend to excel," I reply with a casual shrug.

"That was not meant as a compliment," he growls.

"And that was sarcasm," I fire back, and then belatedly add, "Deputy Chief Torres."

I'm sitting in a boardroom on the eighth floor of Seattle PD Headquarters, otherwise known as the Ice Palace, overlooking downtown. I'm here for yet another reprimand. This time, though, is more of a dog and pony show than I'm used to. They rolled out all the brass for this one: Deputy Chief Torres, Captain Deanna Lewis, Lieutenant Anthony Washington, and my watch commander, Sergeant Terri Welsh, all sit across the table from me, stony faced and silent. It's a superfluous show of force meant to intimidate me with their dour, disapproving glares. They're there to reinforce the gravity of what I've done.

It's cute that they think trotting me out in front of the department heavyweights is enough to rattle me. I know I was in the right, and that's good enough for me. But for paper pushers like these clowns— people who haven't been on the streets in as many years as I've been alive— it's all about perception and politics.

Torres motions to a younger woman in the corner of the room. She picks up a remote and punches a button, then sets it back down on the table as she turns back to her stenograph. Apparently, bureaucracy demands both an oral and a written account of this utterly ridiculous sideshow.

"All right, we are on the record now," Torres begins. "Detective Arrington, you are reminded once again that you are permitted to have outside counsel or your union rep here to advocate on your behalf."

"Noted and waived," I say. "Let's get on with this."

"Very well. Detective Arrington, you are before us today because you struck your superior officer, one Detective Sergeant Matthew Schreiber," Torres says. "What do you have to say for yourself?"

I fold my hands together on the table before me and lean forward so the mic can pick my voice up easier.

"First of all, I wouldn't call Detective Sergeant Schreiber 'superior' in any sense of the word."

Although I see Sergeant Welsh stifle a chuckle, the temperature in the boardroom feels like it just dropped ten degrees. I already see how this is going to go, so I don't really care about making the proper and appropriate impression. This is nothing more than them crossing their T's and dotting their I's as bureaucracy demands. Might as well get my licks in while I can. If I'm going down, I'm going down swinging.

"Do you think this is all a joke, Detective?" Torres seethes.

"Actually, I do," I reply. "I think it's a joke that I'm being hauled in here before you all and Schreiber gets a pat on the back for what he did."

"You were the one who struck D.S. Schreiber, Detective Arrington," Captain Lewis reminds me.

"True. But I would not have needed to do so had he not escalated the situation to that point," I counter.

"A situation of your own creation, Detective," Torres interrupts. "After all, Detective Schreiber would not have confronted you if you had not disobeyed a direct order—"

"A ridiculously stupid order."

"Yours is not to question the orders of your superior—"

"Even when I know they're wrong?"

"That is not for you to say, Detective Arrington."

I lean back in my chair and let out a breath. The air

in the boardroom is crackling with a taut, angry tension. Torres, Washington, and Lewis all glare at me like they want nothing more than to come across the table and beat me bloody. The only friendly face in the room is Welsh, and she already told me there was nothing she could do to help.

I don't blame her. In her spot, I wouldn't want to get ground up in the gears of police politics either. There's no use in her throwing her own career into the meat grinder to save me. Not when this hearing is nothing more than a farce anyway.

"If I had followed D.S. Schreiber's order to remain at the tape line and continue canvassing witnesses, a triple murderer named Adam Barnes would have gotten away," I say. "And correct me if I'm wrong, but are we not in the business of putting men like that behind bars?"

"You can't know for certain that Barnes would have gotten away," Washington counters.

I arch my eyebrow at him. "With all due respect, Lieutenant, you and I both know that D.S. Schreiber is not exactly a— physical specimen," I say. "Barnes is younger and far more athletic. There is no doubt he would have gotten away had I not acted."

"You know, you're continuing to insult D.S. Schreiber is not helping your case," Captain Lewis interjects.

"I am not insulting him, I am merely stating a fact," I respond. "Detective Sergeant Schreiber is in his fifties, he's a smoker, a heavy drinker, and he is at least fifty pounds overweight—"

"Enough, Detective," Torres snaps. "D.S. Schreiber's physical fitness is not in question here today—"

"Perhaps it should be," I comment. "Or perhaps about the physical fitness requirements of the SPD as a whole."

"It is your attitude, Detective," Torres says. "An attitude that has seen you written up nearly a dozen times and suspended once in your career. If not for the intervention of Commissioner Gray, you would have never gotten your shield. I certainly never would have given it to a malcontent like you."

"Sorry, was that a question?" I ask.

Torres' typical pettiness shines through once more. He just had to get it on the record that former Chief Gray promoted me, likely with the hope that my fall from grace will somehow tarnish the reputation of Gray, who is now the Commissioner.

Conventional wisdom says I should keep my mouth shut, listen to what they have to say, then tell them what they want to hear. I've never been good about adhering to the conventional wisdom though. Plus, they're just plain wrong. The truth is, I've grown tired of the bureaucratic bull and the politics of the job. I joined the police department because I wanted to make a difference. I wanted to help people.

But the bloom has definitely been off that particular

rose for quite a while now. And frankly, at the moment, I don't care whether or not they suspend or fire me. I think I'm pretty well done here. I mean, it's not like I need the job or anything. I've got money. This has always been more of a hobby or passion project for me. The desire to help people and be a positive force for change was instilled into me by my late wife. That's why I joined up in the first place. And if they won't let me be a positive force for change in this world, what's the point of being a cop at all?

"Detective Arrington, do you know what your problem is?" Torres growls.

"Constantly being surrounded by imbeciles like Detective Sergeant Schreiber?"

Torres clenches his jaw and exchanges glances with the others, and his expression darkens as he glares at me. If looks could kill, I would be dead ten times over already.

"It's that. Right there," Torres says through gritted teeth. "That attitude. You always think you're the smartest man in the room."

"In almost every case, that has turned out to be true," I egg him on. "No more true than as it relates to D.S. Schreiber."

"Gentlemen, we are getting far afield here, and this is proving counterproductive," Captain Lewis says. "Detective Arrington, as it relates to the incident with D.S. Schreiber, if you would please tell us your story in your own words."

I sigh and pinch the bridge of my nose, trying to stave off the headache that's coming on. Raising my head, I look at each of the people seated across from me in turn, hoping I'm conveying the proper level of contempt I'm feeling for these proceedings with my eyes.

"As I stated in my report, I arrived on the scene of a homicide in the Morris building. Detective Sergeant Schreiber ordered me to secure the police line, assist with crowd control, and interview potential witnesses, which I did," I tell them. "As they worked the crime scene inside, I noticed a man behaving suspiciously. I contacted D.S. Schreiber and asked if he wanted me to detain the man. He said no."

"Because at the time, you had no reason to suspect Mr. Barnes of anything, isn't that correct, Detective Arrington?" Washington adds. "Nothing but your gut."

The corner of my mouth curls upward. "Half of police work is based on your gut, Lieutenant," I say. "You might recall that if you ever stepped out of your ivory tower."

Washington's face twists into a mask of outrage, but Torres puts a hand on his arm, defusing the man's anger. Sort of. Torres turns to me with an expression of utter contempt on his face.

"Go on, Detective," he snaps.

"The man was wearing a hat and jacket, but underneath he matched the exact description from the 9-1-1 call of the suspect. Specifically, I noticed a tattoo on his right wrist that he had missed covering up with the sleeve of his jacket. As I approached to question him, he tried to disappear into the crowd, but I tailed him," I go on. "I was able to move through the crowd and detain the suspect before he broke through."

"So you left your assigned station and took it upon yourself to detain who you merely thought was Mr. Barnes," Washington presses. "The crowd rushed the building and nearly compromised the investigation because you abandoned your post."

"I did. But I would do it again. I had a strong suspicion that this man was Mr. Barnes, and I feared he would kill again. It turns out I was right. He was Adam Barnes, who had committed the three homicides in the Morris building."

"And when D.S. Schreiber confronted you—"

"You mean when D.S. Schreiber verbally accosted me," I correct him. "And put his hands on me first."

"Detective Schreiber admits that he poked you in the chest with his index finger," Lewis jumps in.

"That is incorrect. After spewing a litany of curses on me and insulting every member of my family," I say, "he gave me a two-handed shove in the chest."

"That's not what he says," Torres spits.

"Then he's a liar."

"Nobody can corroborate your account," Lewis says.

"Not surprising," I say.

"So let's just assume that you're right. That Schreiber is lying," Torres goes on.

"I'm right. He is lying," I fire back. "Don't forget that I have hyperthymesia. I don't forget things."

Torres' face darkens. "Even if he did shove you, do you actually consider delivering two punches to the face to be an equal and appropriate response?"

"Yes. If you put your hands on another man, you should expect a response. If you don't, you are not very bright," I say flatly. "Which brings me back to one of my original complaints about D.S. Schreiber."

"I think we've heard enough," Torres says.

"Of course you have," I reply. "But let's not pretend the result of this exercise wasn't predetermined anyway."

Silence descends over the room, and nobody will meet my eyes— except for Torres, who's staring at me with eyes that are gleaming like a kid on Christmas morning. But of course he is. He's been on my back from the jump because he doesn't think somebody like me, who comes from my background, should be allowed to join the force or something. It seems ridiculous that a Deputy Chief had singled me out from the very start, when I was riding in a patrol car, and has harassed and tormented me for the entirety of my career. But he did. Ever since we crossed paths when I was at the academy, and he figured out who I am— or rather, who my family is— he's had a hard-on for me.

"Detective Arrington, over your time with the SPD, you have developed a track record of defying authority and insubordination," he intones. "And now, you've struck a superior officer. We have no choice but to terminate you effective immediately. And I intend to have you stripped of any pension benefits you have accrued."

"Your intelligence could have made you a first-rate detective, Pax," Captain Lewis says. "But your arrogance and that inherent belief you have that you're better than anybody else proved to be your undoing. It's a shame."

A grin curls my lips upward. "In the spirit of all this honesty, let me just say that the constant backstabbing politics within this department, particularly among those of you at the top of the hierarchy, is costing people their lives," I tell them. "It makes you sloppy, unfocused, and largely ineffective as a police force. And that is to the detriment of every citizen of this city. That you choose to focus on me punching Schreiber rather than the fact that we got a killer off the streets is proof of that. That you coddle those who suck up to you in just the right way, rather than the cops who bust their backs and put in the work, those who are good police, is more proof."

"Are you done?" Torres glowers.

"Yeah, I think that about covers it," I say as I get to my feet.

I take the badge and gun off my belt and toss them onto the table, where they land with a hard thud. I would have thought I'd feel something about losing my badge and the career I've had for the last decade, but the truth is, the only thing I feel is relief. Which should tell me everything I need to know.

"All right everybody," I shrug. "It's been fun."

I turn and walk out of the room, then out of police HQ for the last time, my head held high and feeling pretty good about myself.

Arrington Residence; Laurelhurst, WA

"It's for the best, darling," my mother Jessica says. "And now that you have that out of your system, you are free to take your rightful place at the head of the company. Where you should have been all along."

"Agreed," adds my brother George after a brief hesitation. "It's good to have you back, Pax."

And just like that, all of the good feelings I had walking out of HQ disappear like a puff of smoke on the breeze. I have no idea why I came to my family home after being fired. I don't even think it was a conscious decision. I just got in my car and ended up here rather than going home or somewhere else. I really wish now that I hadn't been on autopilot.

We're sitting on the back deck having lunch. Well, George and I are eating. My mom is sipping on what is probably her third martini of the day. The afternoon sky is littered with gray clouds that are growing darker with the whispered promise of rain on the breeze. But for now, the day is relatively warm.

"I'm not back," I tell them. "Just because I'm not working for SPD anymore, doesn't mean I'm thinking about coming back to Archton, or that I don't already have other ideas about what I want to do."

George looks at me curiously. "You already have something else going on?"

"Dear, your father will be so disappointed," my mother frowns. "You know how much he wants you to come work for the family company."

"He'll get over it. As he has for the last decade," I tell her. "George will be great in the role. He's got a real passion for it. I don't."

There's been a wall of ice between me and my father ever since I decided to forgo working for the family's media company in favor of becoming a cop. He said he didn't understand it, and couldn't respect it, which helped open the rift between us. My brother wants the top spot though. He's always coveted it, ever since we were kids. When I told him I was going to be a cop instead, he'd been thrilled with my decision, knowing it cleared the field for him to take over at the top of the Archton Media food chain when my father finally steps down.

Now that I'm not a detective anymore, I know my brother is nervous that I'm going to change my mind about working at Archton. He's been learning the ropes under our father, but he's very clearly the second choice. If I told my father I was coming to work for Archton, I have no doubt that he would push George into some meaningless role with a fancy-yet-serious-sounding title with no real responsibilities. And George knows it too.

"What do you have going on?" he presses, sounding hopeful. "I mean, you just got fired today."

"It's something I've been thinking about for a little while," I reply.

"What is it?"

"Don't worry about it," I tell him. "I'll tell you when you need to know. And right now, you don't need to know."

"Paxton, there is no need to speak to your brother that way," my mother admonishes me.

"Look, I just don't want you thinking I'm trying to encroach on your territory, George," I say. "As far as I'm concerned, Archton is your baby. You've got the desire to do the job that I never had. I mean, come one, you used to hang posters of Citizen Kane and Ted Turner on your walls as a kid. You always wanted to be the big-time media man."

"That's not true." George's face flushes scarlet because he knows it's true.

"I really think you should talk to your father," my mother chimes in.

From the corner of my eye, I can see my brother stiffen and his face darken. I'm sure it makes him feel like garbage to have my mother and father trying so hard to convince me to take the job he feels is rightfully his. It's something that's always made me feel sorry for him since it's a constant reminder to him that he's number two. A constant reminder that he— at least in their eyes — will always live in my shadow.

"I'll speak with Father," I finally relent. "If only to tell him I'm not coming to work at Archton."

"Keep an open mind, dear," she says. "That's all I'm asking."

I drop my napkin onto the table and get to my feet. "Thank you for lunch, Mother," I sigh. "But I need to go."

I pat my brother on the shoulder as I walk off the deck and leave the house, my good mood spoiled. My family is good at doing that. Always has been.

ONE
REUBEN HAYES

Bel Air, CA

I watch from the window of the abandoned building as the white Escalade pulls into the empty parking lot. Given how many of them I've seen in her neighborhood, it's apparently the new soccer mom's vehicle of choice. I raise the night vision binoculars to my eyes and watch as Mrs. Elena Henderson steps out of the vehicle and looks around, wringing her hands together nervously.

I turn my binoculars to the old, ratty Toyota Camry I stole that's parked across the street and can see the cardboard box on the back seat. I can't see the bundle inside, but I'm sure it's there. This is the part I hate most about my admittedly unusual lifestyle. I consider it barbaric and uncivilized. But there is, unfortunately, nothing I can do about it. I have work I must do, and that requires money. Which makes this a tasteless but necessary chore.

I open the cell phone I picked up at the market earlier and switch on my voice modulator. When I see the green light showing it's active, I punch in Mrs. Henderson's phone number, and with the phone pressed to my ear, I watch her through the binoculars. She is an exquisite creature. Tall, thin, long, lustrous blonde hair, icy blue eyes, and a smattering of freckles across the bridge of her nose. She could be a supermodel.

"Yes, hello?" she answers the phone, panic in her voice. "I'm here. I've done what you said."

She has. From my vantage point, I can see she's come alone, and there are no cops in the area that I can see. She and her husband never called the police and have done everything I've asked. These types of people always do.

"Yes you have, Mrs. Henderson. You're a very good, very brave woman," I tell her. "And you brought the money?"

"I—I did."

"Let me see it, please."

She quickly reaches into the car and pulls out a bag. It's large and heavy, and I can see her struggling with it. It hits the ground, and she kneels and curses under her breath, trying to hold the phone between her chin and shoulder. She fumbles with the zipper for a moment before she manages to get it open, spreading it wide. I peer closely at it through the binoculars and see the bundles of cash inside. So far, so good.

"One hundred thousand," she stammers. "Just like you asked for."

It's a hefty sum but will hardly make much of a dent in her husband's bank account. My goal is not to bleed these people dry but make just enough to sustain me. I'm not a greedy man. I consider greed to be a foul and distasteful quality in a person. It's... rude. And I place a high value on manners and decorum since I've always believed that poor manners are a sign of poor breeding.

"That is very good, Mrs. Henderson," I say. "You have done well. Thank you."

"So do I get my son back now?" she asks frantically. "Do I get my Toby back?"

"Yes of course," I tell her. "I am a man of my word. I abhor lying."

"Wh—where is he?" she pleads. "Where is he?"

"All in due time, Mrs. Henderson," I reply. "I need to make certain that I secure my payment without incident."

"Please, please, let me have my son. I've done everything you asked."

"And so long as you continue doing that, everything will turn out fine," I say. "And we can put this whole disagreeable mess behind us."

She lets out a choked sob, the fear for her son's safety keeping her from forming anything resembling a coherent sentence. It's understandable, of course. A mother's fear for her child is primal. Visceral.

"Now, drive to the corner of Surrey and Fourth and pull to the curb," I instruct her. "I will call and give you the location of your son."

"Please. Tell me where—"

"Surrey and Fourth, Mrs. Henderson," I cut her off. "Get into your vehicle and drive there now, please."

The time it will take her to get to the location I've given will give me enough time to get across the street, grab the bag, and get away cleanly, the funds to continue my work secured for another year. Truthfully, it's more than enough for a year with the excess going to my retirement fund. Over the years, I have put together quite a nest egg, and once I am ready to walk away from this life and my work, I will be able to live well. I think I deserve that.

"Mrs. Henderson, I do not like having to repeat myself. I won't ask you again," I press. "Please close the bag, get into your car, and drive to the corner of Surrey and Fourth."

She hesitates for a moment but finally relents and does what I say. She zips up the bag and clambers into her car, her tires chirping on the pavement as she takes off quickly. Knowing I have only minutes to act, I throw my binoculars into my backpack and descend the stairs quickly. I step into the cool night air and cross the street, picking up the bag, before retreating to the second car I have stashed around the corner. I toss it into the trunk and climb behind the wheel.

I start the engine and then use the burner phone to make my call to Mrs. Henderson. I redial the number and hold it to my ear. She picks it up before the first ring even ends.

"Where is my son?"

"You will find him in a yellow Honda Civic across the street from the old Majestic Building. The car is locked, and the key is under the front drivers' side wheel well," I tell her. "It was a pleasure doing business with you, Mrs. Henderson. Be well."

I disconnect the call and break the burner in half before throwing it out the window. I put my car in gear and drive off, cutting down side streets, following my route until I make it to the highway. I turn up the volume on my stereo, drumming my fingers on the steering wheel in time with Duran Duran's song "Planet Earth", feeling good. Feeling great, actually. I've always loved eighties music. It fills my soul with something close to happiness. Or as close as I get to it. There is just something so pure and innocent about it.

And as I drive home, my thoughts turn to Elena Henderson. She is beautiful. A goddess made flesh. Marcus Henderson is not worthy of her, and he certainly does not deserve such a remarkable creature. Not that I am any more worthy, but it's a shame she did not find somebody who deserves her.

Elena Henderson is a former beauty queen. Miss

Nebraska 2009. She is bright, articulate, and passionate. And she is the current trophy wife of Marcus Henderson, one of the slimiest celebrity attorneys in Los Angeles. If you're a movie star who runs afoul of the law, Marcus Henderson is the man to sweep it all under the rug and make it disappear. The Henderson's laugh it up with studio execs and big-time producers at black-tie galas practically every week.

I know everything there is to know about Elena. And about her family. I've been watching them for months now. Getting to know them. Memorizing their routines. Collecting every bit of information I could about them, all in preparation for tonight's activities. And now that it's done and my immediate future is secured, and I no longer have to sully myself with the distasteful practice of ransoming money out of terrified parents, I can focus on my work once more. My real work. My passion, really.

But the more I think about her, the deeper she burrows into my mind. I literally cannot stop thinking about Elena as I drive home. Every other thought is flushed out of my head, and I can't seem to stop seeing images of her face in my mind. She is perfection, and I would love to add her to my collection.

I don't normally do what I'm thinking about right now. I have a thing about going back to the same well again since, statistically speaking, it increases the odds that I get caught. I've been very disciplined and rigid in my planning and execution and never deviate from my plans unless it is absolutely necessary. That's why I've been able to operate for more than twenty years unimpeded.

I pull my car up to the guard shack and lower the window as I turn the volume down on my stereo. The guard, a doughy, pale, but pleasant enough man steps out of the booth and flashes me a smile.

"Heard you comin' a block away," he says.

"What can I say, Robert? I enjoy the classics," I reply. "You should give them a try sometime."

He nods. "I'll do that," he says with a grin and presses a button on his remote. "You have a good night, Mr. Hayes."

"You as well, Robert."

I drive through the gate and follow the streets through the tract homes. Everything so normal. Staid. Nothing out of the ordinary ever happens here, and everything can usually be anticipated. Planned for. It's one of the things I love most about this housing community. The predictability.

As I pull into my driveway, I see Elena Henderson's face once again. Maybe this once. Maybe I can go back to that well this one time. Just this once. Surely, she has some sin that she needs to be cleansed of.

TWO
PAXTON

Four Months Later...

Arrington Investigations; Downtown Seattle

I watch the workman leave after he finishes hanging the burnished metal sign emblazoned with my company logo on the far wall. I take a moment to admire it and nod. It's sharp. Adds a little gravitas to this operation.

"I think that's it," I say. "We are officially open for business."

"I think that calls for a drink then."

Brody Singer— Broderick to his parents— produces a bottle of scotch and a pair of glasses, sets them down on my desk, and pours out a couple of drinks for us. He hands me one and raises his own. I tap my glass against his.

"To the grand opening of Arrington Investigations," Brody says.

"To the best investigative team since Sherlock and Watson," I reply.

Brody laughs. "You know Watson was the brains behind that dynamic duo, don't you?" he says.

I wave him off with a laugh. "They each had their own strengths and contributed in their own way."

"Yeah, but Watson was the brains."

I laugh then take a long swallow of my scotch. Brody's been my best friend since prep school and is closer to me than my own brother. After the SPD fired me, I told him I was thinking about opening my own investigative firm, and he was all in from the jump. I was still waffling for weeks. But it was Brody who actually pushed me to pull the trigger and do it.

He's been floundering about since we graduated from college, with no real sense of what he wanted to do with his life. He's traveled the world as he searched for himself and finally went to work for his father's financial firm for lack of anything else that interested him. And when he finally talked me into this, he couldn't get this office set up fast enough, so I let him locate an office and design its set up.

We occupy the top floor of a small red brick office building, and the elevator opens straight into our lobby area. It's a loft-style office with an open floor plan done in red brick and dark, hard woods. There are three large arching windows in the back wall, giving us a clear view of the Cascade Mountain range and the iconic Space Needle. We both have offices on opposite sides of the loft; both of them made of three walls of clear glass against the brick. There is enough space that we have room for two more offices should we ever expand, and a glass-encased meeting room with a long table, apparently for meetings with our non-existent staff. A kitchenette, outfitted with all the latest gadgets, sits tucked away in a corner.

The office is decorated with vintage photos of Seattle, framed and mounted, hung on the walls. It's a touch of old Seattle done with a modern flair. I like it. I like it a lot.

"You know, you have a real future in interior design if you wanted to go that way," I tell him.

He chuckles. "Yeah, I'll keep that in mind in case I ever get tired of you."

"That shouldn't take long," comes a female voice. "I give it a month. Tops."

I turn and see Blake Wilder sauntering into the office, a wide smile on her face. She works out of the FBI's Seattle field office, but she rarely seems to be in the area. Blake steps over and pulls me into a warm embrace. I met Blake at an anti-terrorism seminar a few years back, and we struck up what some consider an unlikely friendship. Local cops and Feds don't typically get along, but Blake's different. She doesn't throw her FBI creds around like they make her better than anybody, and she never tries to bigfoot her way onto a case.

Blake is just a good, decent person who's more interested in doing her job and getting results than in chasing headlines or making a name for herself. She's a straight shooter who doesn't take crap from anybody, and a very good agent to boot. I've got a lot of respect for her. Veronica, my late wife, was really fond of her. They were friends. And after Veronica passed, it was Blake who helped me through the grief. She was always there to talk to, to listen to me, and to offer advice. Blake was always just there whenever I needed her.

"A month?" I ask. "Do you have that little faith in me?"

She scoffs. "It's not a lack of faith. I just know how much of a jerk you are," she replies. "How Brody's been able to put up with you for as long as he has is a mystery to me."

"Lots and lots of this," Brody points to his glass, taking an exaggerated swig.

"Screw you both," I fire back with a laugh. "It's good to see you, Blake."

"Good to see you are landing on your feet after getting the shaft from PD," she says. "Sorry I didn't call sooner. I had this task force I was part of—"

I wave her off. "You don't need to apologize," I say. "You're a big rock star Fed. You don't need to explain yourself to us mere mortals."

She laughs. "Shut up, Arrington."

I grab a glass from the sideboard and pour her out a few fingers of scotch and hand it over. She takes it and taps it against my glass and takes a swallow, a slow smile creeping across her face.

"I'll say one thing for you rich boys," she notes. "You sure do drink the good stuff. A bottle of this stuff would probably cost me a year's salary."

"Right. I know what you Feds make," I grin. "And it's not like you came from a poor family yourself there, Wilder."

She takes another swallow of her drink and nods. "Maybe not, but I still don't have a ten-figure trust fund."

I chuckle. "Please. It's eight figures, at best," I correct her. "Remember, I have to split it up with a couple of siblings."

"Whatever you say, Arrington," she rolls her eyes. "So what's the division of labor around here? I mean, when you actually have a paying client come through the door, that is."

"If you build it, they will come," I offer. "We'll have clients. We'll have to fight them off with a stick soon enough."

"You sound so sure of yourself," Blake remarks. "But

then, I suppose that shouldn't surprise me. If there's one thing you're not short of, it's confidence."

"People need quality investigative work," I reply. "More than that, we can do things and go places SPD can't go."

"Yeah well, just be sure you're not breaking any laws when you're doing your quality investigative work," she reminds me.

"I'll do my best."

"As far as the division of labor goes, I do all the work, and Pax here is going to take all the credit," Brody chimes in.

"That sounds about right," Blake says.

"You're both regular comedians," I reply. "To answer your question, Blake, Brody's specialty is tech, so he's going to be doing the computer work, and I'll be in the field."

"So basically, I'll be doing all the work," Brody grins. "And he'll be taking all the credit."

Brody's phone rings and he pulls it out of his pocket, a slow grin spreading across his face.

"I recognize that look," I say. "What's her name?"

"Jeanine," he says. "Or Madeline. I don't remember offhand."

He heads out of my office and answers the call, making Blake rolls her eyes as a chuckle bubbles out of her throat.

"I see some things haven't changed," she chirps.

"You know, one of these days, all those girls are gonna unionize against him."

"Yeah, he's still grazing at the buffet of life," I note.

"Come on," she says. "Let's get out of here and get a drink."

"Sounds good to me."

THREE

The Pulpit; Downtown Seattle

"So what were you doing on the task force?" I ask.

"Gunrunners," she replies. "Had a complicated multi-state network going on."

"Did you get them?"

"Have you ever known me to not get somebody I went after?"

I chuckle. "And you say I'm full of confidence."

"No, I say you're full of crap," she counters. "There's a difference."

We're sitting in a bar down the street from our office called The Pulpit. It's an old church building that was abandoned and has been converted into a neighborhood tavern. Rather than demolish the building and construct something new, the new owners of the building left all of the original architecture in place. The Pulpit retains all of the soaring arches and Gothic details of the church, even the large stained-glass windows.

They also repurposed all of the original wood and furnishings in the place to build their bar. The pews have been cut and used to make the booths, and the raised dais that held the altar is now the stage for live music. The acoustics in this place are amazing. I thought reusing and repurposing of all the materials inside the church was pretty clever actually. This place definitely has an atmosphere you won't find in most bars.

"Isn't this place a little... sacrilegious?" Blake asks as she eyeballs the waitresses dressed in a rather risqué nun's habits.

I shrug. "If you're uptight about it, I suppose," I grin, then snap my fingers. "Oh that's right; you're Catholic. Being uptight is natural to you."

"You're such a jerk," she laughs.

Our waitress, May, stops at our table and flashes me a smile. It falters slightly when her eyes fall on Blake, but she recovers quickly. May's a cute, shapely brunette who's been trying to get me to ask her out for a while now.

"Well hey Pax," she says. "How ya doin' today?"

"Doing good," I nod. "How about yourself?"

"I'm good, sweetie," she says. "What can I get you?"

"I'll have the usual," I say with a grin. "Blake here is going to have a Bloody Pope."

Blake looks at me with wide eyes and a crooked grin on her face. May gives her another look, and it's not hard to see the coldness in her eyes. But she turns back to me and is all smiles once more.

"Sure thing," she says. "Be right back with your drinks."

"Thanks, May."

"Cute girl," Blake says. "I think she's got a crush."

"It's harmless," I tell her. "Besides, I think you intimidate her."

She scoffs and rolls her eyes. "That's ridiculous," she replies. "But if you ever order for me again like that, I'll show you how intimidating I can be."

I quirk a grin at her and wink. It's easy to see why a girl like May would be intimidated by Blake. She carries herself well, like the strong, accomplished woman she is. The Bureau is a man's world, and if you're a woman, the only way to thrive is to be as tough, if not tougher, than the men you're dealing with. And Blake is thriving.

Add to that the fact that she's a knockout. She's five-nine, with strawberry blonde hair and green eyes that sparkle like polished emeralds. Her body is somehow both curvy and rock-solid with muscle. She wouldn't be out of place as a swimsuit model. She's smart as a whip, too. There aren't many people who can keep up with me, but Blake is definitely one of them. She's the complete package and has an air of confidence about her that is undeniable.

"So what is a Bloody Pope anyway?"

"It's kind of like a White Russian with a drizzle of grenadine in it."

"And you thought I'd like it, why exactly?"

I shrug. "I just wanted to add to your sacrilegious experience here at The Pulpit."

"So kind of you," she laughs.

May drops off our drinks a moment later and scampers off after eyeballing Blake coolly one last time.

"She should really just piss on your leg and get it over with," she says.

"Don't give her any ideas."

I watch as Blake raises the glass, studying the creamy white liquid with the swirl of grenadine red in it. She frowns, looking at it like it's a snake, coiled and ready to strike her. But she gamely takes a sip of her drink, and her expression changes. The frown disappears, and she smiles.

"It's actually not half bad," she admits. "Sacrilegious, but not bad."

"So I'm guessing you don't want to try the Crucified Man? It's served with a skewered cocktail weenie as a garnish."

"That's nasty. And don't push your luck," she laughs. "So how are you doing, Pax? I mean really."

I take a sip of my scotch and nod. "I'm good, actually."

"Yeah?" she replies. "I know how you feel about change and losing your gig with PD is a pretty big change."

"I'm working on that," I admit. "But truth be told, I

think getting out of the SPD might be one of the best things that could have happened for me."

"How so?"

"Because now I don't have to deal with all of the politics. I don't have to worry about 'fellow officers' riding me because they don't know how to investigate the way I can," I say. "I'm free to get results now, without having to worry about somebody else second-guessing my actions. And since I don't have to stick to the rules as a detective anymore, that opens up a whole new line of communication with anyone who doesn't want to deal with the SPD. I'm accountable to no one but myself."

"So basically the leash is off, and you're free to be your cocky self," she grins. "Well, more so than you were already anyway."

"You— and the department apparently— call it having an attitude," I offer. "I simply call it cutting through the crap and getting to the truth of the matter."

She laughs. "You need to learn to play the game."

"I detest the game," I respond. "The game is why we have so many problems in society. If people would just be honest enough to speak the truth—"

"Nobody wants to hear the truth," she cuts me off. "Oh, they say they do. But they don't. Not really."

"That's why I think people are idiots."

"And that's why I can count the number of friends you have on one hand," she grins. "And have fingers left over."

"Yeah well, I've always preferred quality over quantity anyway."

She takes another drink and settles back into the booth. "So why go the PI route?" she asks. "I mean, with your resources, you could do anything you wanted to. But you're going to spend your time chasing down deadbeat dads and unfaithful spouses? I can't see it."

"Would you believe me if I said I was obsessed with Sherlock Holmes when I was growing up?" I ask. "I read my first Holmes book at eight-years-old."

"Sure, I'd believe it," she replies. "Obsessive is your personality type. You don't know how to do anything in moderation."

I chuckle. "I loved the books, and because of them, I always thought I'd make a top-notch investigator," I continue. "And aside from Veronica pushing me in that direction, it's one reason I ended up joining the SPD. I wanted to make detective and start investigating real crimes. Make a real difference."

Blake nods. "I can see the similarities between you and Holmes," she grins. "Both arrogant. Condescending. You both always think you're right and everybody else is a moron."

"And more times than not, I'm proven correct," I shrug.

She laughs. "Fine. But tell me why you want to be a PI," she presses. "It has got to be about more than just your childhood love of the books."

A small smile touches the corners of my mouth as the thoughts go swirling through my mind, inevitably landing on images of Veronica, as they usually do. Even in death, she's still my guiding light. My Northern Star. Everything I do is with the hope that she'd approve and perhaps, even be proud of me. Even in death, her influence on me is strong.

Before I met Veronica, I was shiftless. Aimless. I had no real sense of purpose or direction and was just sort of wandering through life with no real thought to my future. When you come from the kind of family I did, you never really had to think about it.

But when I met Veronica, that all changed. She taught me all about my privilege and how I was in a position to make a positive impact in this world. She'd come from very little and had worked her way up on her own merits. Everything she had, she earned. She believed very strongly in serving others and doing right in her community.

And it's because of her that I started to think about joining the police force in the first place. She inspired me. She moved me. She actually got me thinking about my life in terms of how I can help others, rather than just living my life for myself. Selfishly. And without regard for others.

"I'll admit, I am hoping it's not all cheating husbands and wives," I laugh. "I hope there's some actual detective work in there too. A chance to make a real difference."

"But why?" she asks. "When the whole world is your oyster— as it so clearly is— why do it?"

I let out a long breath, then drain my glass and signal to May for another round of scotch for the both of us. Blake's only halfway through her Bloody Pope, but I know she can drink with the best of them and will be ready for another soon enough.

"Veronica really got under my skin all those years ago. Made me appreciate what I have and where I come from," I tell her. "But more importantly, what sort of a difference I can make. She made me believe in service and giving back to the community. Doing what I can to make it a better place."

"That sounds like you should be running for office, not becoming a PI. That's a political stump speech," Blake grins. "It's a beautiful speech, don't get me wrong, but tell me why you're really doing this."

A faint smile flickers across my lips. That's Blake. I can always count on her to give it to me straight and not sugarcoat things. She and I are a lot alike in that way. The biggest difference is that she knows how to play politics. She just seems to inherently know how to smooth over the ruffled feathers and say the right thing at the right time. It's a skill I never cared to learn. But then, I'm not a woman trying to make my way up the ladder in the Bureau either, so I guess it's just another example of my privilege showing.

"Seriously, have you met me? I can't kiss babies or glad-hand with donors. My personality is a bit too..."

"Rude and abrasive?"

"Yeah. But I guess that honestly, it's kind of my way of keeping Veronica's spirit alive with the tools that I have. By helping others like she would, I feel like I'm keeping her alive in my heart. Like I was doing as a detective," I say softly. "That's about the best way I can put it."

May drops off our round of drinks and gives me a smile before turning around and sashaying away again. Blake and I lapse into silence for a long moment as she absorbs what I said.

"That's beautiful, Pax," she finally says. "It really is."

I give her a tight smile and look down into my drink. I'm not big on opening up and sharing my feelings with anybody. But I've always felt comfortable with Blake. I don't even feel comfortable enough with Brody to share the things I've shared with her. Probably because of what we went through together when Veronica died, I feel bonded to her in a way. With her, I feel safe enough to open up.

"And here I honestly didn't think you had a sensitive, sentimental bone in your entire body," she says. "In fact, I didn't know you had emotions at all."

I can see her trying to stifle the smile that's flickering across her lips. It's a fight she loses, though, when she erupts in a fit of laughter that echoes all around The Pulpit, drawing the eyes of the patrons to us. Like I said, the acoustics in here are pretty amazing.

"And you say I'm a jerk," I laugh along with her.

"That's because you are."

"Or maybe I'm the normal one," I argue. "And everybody else is a jerk."

She arches her eyebrow at me, a grin twisting her lips. "Yeah, you keep believing that."

FOUR

Arrington Investigations; Downtown Seattle

Arrington Investigations has been officially open for three weeks now, and the only people who've come through the door are the Postmates guy, a man who was lost and on the wrong floor, a woman who wanted to drop off some religious literature, and an eight-year-old girl who wanted me to find her cat. I did technically end up finding it, but only because it happened to be in her own front yard once I drove her home.

Suffice it to say, we haven't gotten off to the booming start I'd anticipated, and I'm not doing much in the way of service to the community. Not as much as I'd hoped.

I stand at the windows looking out over the expanse of the city, wondering what I need to do to get my name out there and get people coming through the door who need help. It's not a money thing. It's more of a pride thing, really. That I haven't had one legitimate client in three weeks of operation is bothering me. I want to help people and make Veronica proud by carrying on her legacy.

She was a journalist who worked for the Seattle Times for a couple of years. But she couldn't seem to get off the community spotlight desk and felt stifled. She thought she could do more good investigating and reporting on actual issues that impacted the people, rather than covering chili cook-offs and spelling bees.

So she launched her own investigative journalism website and podcast. She focused on investigating the real issues. It was all still in its infancy, but she was already growing a following after a few short months.

She inspired me to want to be an investigator, too. I had dreams of the two of us as a tag team. Me taking down criminals, her taking down corrupt politicians and exposing scandals. We could have done so much good. But then she died, and all those dreams faded like Seattle mist.

When Blake asked me why I'm pursuing this PI gig, I told her it was to keep Veronica's spirit alive and my love for the old Sherlock Holmes books. Which is entirely true. But that's not the entire story. I refrained from telling her everything, from sharing all of my reasons, simply because I know she would have frowned on it. Knowing her like I do, she probably would have tried to talk me out of it. Or at least poured a bucket of cold water on my enthusiasm.

Officially, Veronica died in a car accident. It was a cold, rainy, January night. The theory is that she hit a patch of black ice and lost control. Her car rolled over four times and landed top side down in a ditch. The medical examiner said she suffered severe head trauma and died quickly. All of the T's crossed, all of the I's dotted.

The trouble is, I don't buy the official story. For a lot of reasons. First, it was cold that night, but it wasn't cold enough to ice the roads over. I pored over the weather reports and all of the pertinent data and cannot force myself to believe there was ice on the road. Second, I made dozens of requests to review the wreckage of the car, but I never got a chance to. It was impounded before I could find anything. The investigators say it was too damaged during the wreck, but I don't buy it. Never have.

Blake's looked over all of the files, and she hasn't found any fault in them. She thinks the investigation was thorough, complete, and the conclusions they came to are correct. I don't want to contradict Blake necessarily, but the conclusions they drew never sat right with me. I've never agreed with the official story.

I've tried for the last couple of years to get somebody to look into the case. To get somebody to take a deep dive into it. But nobody was willing to open the files to take a closer look, and I was shot down at every turn.

And as a relative to the victim, I wasn't allowed to look into it myself. If I'd tried, it was possible I could have found myself in trouble for misconduct and abusing the power of the police for my personal benefit.

But in this new role, free of the constraints of department politics, I can do what I want. I can take a closer look at Veronica's case and not have to worry about politics or having Internal Affairs breathing down my neck for crossing a line I shouldn't have. I can investigate now until I am thoroughly satisfied with the conclusion I draw.

One way or another, I will find out what happened to my wife.

I held that back from Blake. But she's insanely perceptive and probably knows reopening Veronica's case is part of what I'm doing with Arrington Investigations anyway. If she knows, she was good enough not to say anything about it. She's willing to let me do what I need to do and is probably hoping that I'll work this out of my system and eventually come to agree with the official conclusion.

I hear the office door open and turn to see Brody coming through. Immediately, I can tell something's wrong. His face is tight, his expression pensive. He's usually the clown with a smile on his face at all hours of the day, so seeing him look distressed like this tells me that whatever it is can't be good.

"What's up?" I ask. "You okay?"

"We need to talk."

Without another word, I lead him into my office and sit down behind my desk. He drops down into the chair across from me. His body is tense, and he's got a strange look on his face I don't think I've ever seen before.

"Talk to me, man," I tell him. "What's going on?"

"A friend of mine— well, the daughter of a family friend anyway— had her daughter kidnapped," he explains. "Her name is Kayla Morgan, and her daughter is Jordan."

I sit up a little straighter, my interest piqued. For my first case to be a kidnapping has me feeling inappropriately excited. Not that I'll tell Brody that. I'm not that much of an insensitive bastard, regardless of what Blake says. It's just that I actually have a chance to do something good and to genuinely help somebody in need.

"They need somebody to handle this for them quietly," he tells me. "I told her we might be able to help."

"Of course we will," I nod. "We'll help. Let's go talk to her."

FIVE

Morgan Residence; Windermere, WA

She sits across from us on the sofa in the sitting room, a wadded-up tissue in one hand, her husband's hand in the other. They're wearing matching expressions of grief and fear on their faces. When they look at me, I can see the light of hope shining in their eyes. Hope that I can help. That I'll get Jordan back home to them where she belongs.

"I don't know how it happened," Kayla starts, her voice thick with emotion. "We were at the park, and she was playing with some of the other kids while I talked with some of the other mothers. And then she was just—gone."

A choked sob bursts from her throat and she leans her head down on her husband's shoulder. He wraps his arm around his wife and pulls her tightly to him. He strokes her hair softly. Even though I can see the sorrow in his eyes, he's trying to be strong for her.

"It's not your fault," Joseph says. "Don't blame yourself, Kayla."

"Your husband is right, this isn't your fault," I say. "You can't beat yourself up about this. It could have happened to anybody."

I try to inject as much sympathy and compassion into my voice as I can, try to reassure her, but it doesn't come as naturally to me as it does to other people. I often have to simply fake it. I know most people would say that makes me sound like a sociopath, but there's nothing I can do about it. I process emotions differently. And judging by the look on Kayla's face, my words sounded as false coming out of my mouth as they'd felt to speak. I failed to reassure her. I'm not here to reassure them though. I'm here to get their daughter back home to them, safe and unharmed.

As Joseph embraces his wife and smooths her hair as she cries, I clear my throat and look around their home. Windermere is one of Seattle's wealthiest suburbs and is home to many of the one-percent of the one-percenters, which is impressive given the wealth in the area. It's a picturesque place with an almost small town feel to it. The homes are all stately and grand, though the owners do their best to avoid looking gauche or ostentatious. No enormous mansions or palatial estates here. After all, it would be tacky to go flaunting one's wealth in such an obvious way. One must at least keep up the pretense of being humble.

The Morgans are no different. Though everything in their home is obviously expensive, the effect is restrained. Understated. It's feigned humility at its best. I'd know since my family home is in Laurelhurst, which is just up the road. Although not a shoebox and we had more than enough house to move around in, it certainly isn't a grand, palatial estate either. Like the homes in Windermere, my family home is restrained and understated.

Given my upbringing, I can't exactly pretend to be a man of the people or a salt of the earth type, but I think I'm a little more level-headed than most of my family. That's mostly Veronica's influence on me, but working for the SPD for a decade exposed me to things I never would have seen in the staid, sanitized world the Arringtons exist in. That sort of experience can't help but change you. Humble you. Well, as much as I can be humbled anyway.

"Mr. and Mrs. Morgan?"

We all turn to see a tall, thin, severe looking woman in a gray dress with a white apron tied around her waist standing in the doorway of the sitting room. Beyond her, I see a man in dark blue coveralls and a blue ballcap with a cable company logo on it pulled low over his eyes. He's got a tool bag slung over his shoulder and a clipboard in his hand. His mouth is open, and he's gaping around the wide, circular foyer, seemingly impressed with the size and ostentatiousness of the place.

"Yes, what is it, Mercy?" Joseph asks.

"The repairman is finished," she replies. "I just wanted to make sure there was nothing else before I sent him away?"

"No, it's fine," Joseph replies. "Thank you, Mercy."

"Very good, sir."

Mercy walks to the foyer and dismisses the repairman as I turn back to the Morgans. Kayla is a beautiful woman. Dark hair, darker eyes, tall and shapely, and impeccably fashionable. Joseph is a tall, thin man with round, rimless glasses and a receding hairline. His hair is sandy blond, and his eyes are blue.

Sitting side by side, they look like the Homecoming Queen and the class nerd. They're an unlikely couple, but it's not hard to see that even though they are hurting in ways they couldn't have foreseen, they are still very much in love. Some couples handle situations like this by letting their fear consume them and end up tearing each other apart. Usually because one will want to handle the situation one way, while the other wants to go a different direction.

But it seems to have strengthened the bond and the resolve of these two. These two seem to be in lockstep with each other. They're drawing closer, rather than splitting apart. And that's a good thing.

"And how old is Jordan?" I ask.

"She's four," Kayla replies.

"Brody told me the kidnapper contacted you?" I ask.

They nod in unison. "Yes," Kayla says. "It was a man using one of those things that disguised his voice."

"A voice modulator," I note. "Okay, so what did he say?"

"He told me that if we don't follow his instructions to the letter, he would kill Jordan," she says, choking back a sob.

"And what were his instructions?"

Kayla opens her mouth to reply but breaks down into tears, unable to speak. Joseph clears his throat and turns to me.

"He said if we called the police, he would kill our daughter," he says. "No police. He was adamant about that."

It's a common tactic kidnappers for ransom use, so I am unsurprised by it. The fear of something happening to their child will make most any parent pliable and make them adhere to almost anything. It's the ultimate form of control.

"What does he want?" I ask. "What is his main demand?"

"A quarter of a million dollars," Joseph says quietly.

For somebody with the kind of portfolio the Morgans have, I'm sure it's just a drop in the bucket. They can probably fork over that kind of cash without having to worry about skipping a meal. It's curious to me though. The kidnapper obviously knows the Morgans have money; it's likely why he targeted them for an abduction in the first place. And while a quarter of a million is a healthy amount, it's not... excessive. Not by their standards. The demand is almost restrained, in a way. I don't know if it means anything just yet, but it's an interesting piece of information I'll squirrel away to give some thought to later.

"And when does he want it by?" I ask.

"Tomorrow night," Kayla says.

"Where is the drop?"

"He said he'd call with instructions," Joseph says. "Tomorrow night at six. He said promptly at six."

I look over at Brody, who hasn't said a word through this interview and is just sitting there looking shellshocked. I imagine knowing this family and seeing them go through this has to be tough. He's letting me take the lead. The trouble is, I'm not sure where to go with this all just yet.

Over the last few months, I've read up on various investigative techniques, but given that this is my first real case, I'm still finding my footing. But this is what I wanted, and this sort of thing is what I'm good at. I'll figure out the details as I go.

"So am I correct in assuming that you're not going to call the police?" I ask.

They shake their heads in unison. "Not with our daughter's life at stake," Kayla says. "I won't risk her life."

"If a quarter of a million dollars will get Jordan back us safely, it will be worth every penny," Joseph adds.

"Okay, so how can I help you?" I ask.

It seems a fair question since they seem content to pay the ransom and not involve the authorities. It's an approach I don't think is entirely wrong, given all of the bureaucratic red tape and borderline incompetence of the SPD. It seems more likely than not that they'd bungle the response and wind up getting Jordan killed because some idiot like Schreiber would make it more about his ego than getting the job done properly and safely.

"We would like you to make the ransom drop for us," Joseph says.

"And we would like you to learn anything you can about this man when you see him so that we can use it to bring him down later." Kayla clenches her hands into fists, her voice heated. "Brody says you're the best man to do that. After we get our little girl back, I want this man to pay."

"We want to find him when this is all over." Like his wife, Joseph's voice hardens into steel. "Once we have Jordan back safely, I want to find him. Nobody does this to us. Nobody does this to our daughter and gets away with it."

He doesn't have to tell me what it is he wants to find this man for. It's obvious. Once the exchange takes place, and Jordan is back home, I have no doubt that if I am able to discern the man's identity, they'll hire somebody else to execute him. Or hell, maybe they'll even offer the money to me to do it. I can understand the impulse. And in their place, I might want— and do— the same exact thing.

I wonder, though, how that would play for a man who is planning to launch a run for a Congressional seat within the next year. From what I've learned, Joseph Morgan has big ambitions, politically speaking. But that's not for me to judge. Nor is it for me to dictate ethics and morals to these two parents who are scared and angry right now. It's only for me to do the job they need me to do right now.

I nod. "I can do that," I tell them. "I'll be happy to help."

SIX

REUBEN HAYES

Bainbridge Island, WA

"It's time for supper, Jordan," I say. "Grilled cheese and tomato soup."

She looks up at me with wide blue eyes that are red and puffy, swollen, and shimmering with tears, but doesn't speak to me. She hasn't since I lost my temper and yelled at her earlier. She wouldn't stop crying and yelling for her mother. It had gotten to be too much for me to bear, so I snapped and screamed at her to shut up.

I hate losing my temper like that. Yelling and screaming like that is low-rent and classless. It's the sort of thing people without manners do. I am better than that and hold myself to a higher standard.

"I'm sorry I lost my temper earlier, Jordan," I tell

her. "I should not have yelled at you like that, so I apologize if I frightened you."

She looks at me with those wide eyes of hers and sniffs loudly. "I want my mommy."

"Of course you do. And as long as they follow the rules, you will be back with them soon enough," I tell her. "For now, just eat your supper and watch cartoons. If you're a good girl, I'll bring you a pudding cup later."

On the television screen, a dark-haired girl with her pet monkey in red boots runs around, trying to solve a mystery while talking to the audience. I use the remote and raise the volume a bit for her.

"See? That's better, isn't it?" I ask as I set the remote down out of her reach on the tall dresser.

"I want my mommy," she says. "I want my mommy now!"

I see her building to another meltdown and want to prevent another screaming fit. From either of us. I take a deep breath and let it out slowly, giving the girl as warm a smile as I can muster. Which, under the circumstances, is not all that warm.

"Eat your supper," I say.

I back out of the room and close the door then slide the bolt home, locking her in. I walk up the stairs and shut the basement door, bolting that closed as well. After that, I pour a glass of wine and head out onto the back deck as the sun slips toward the horizon, casting the sky in vibrant shades of red and orange. The wispy clouds overhead look to be aflame, and a cool breeze blows in off Puget Sound. In the distance, the Cascades rise high into the air, standing silent sentinel over the world, safeguarding us as they have for millennia.

I hadn't expected that I would need to abduct another child for cash so soon after taking the Henderson child a few months back. But I'd come across an opportunity to better secure my future, so I'd had to dip into my retirement fund to finance it. It was unexpected but necessary. But it left me needing to fill in that dent with another job. I don't want to put myself behind where I want to be when my work is complete, and I'm ready to walk away.

I sit down on the chair and put my feet up on the railing that runs along the wrap-around porch. I take a drink then cradle the wine glass in my hands as I look at the city sitting across the Sound from me and sigh. I take a drink of my wine as I watch one of the last ferries of the day crossing from Seattle.

Unlike the home I have down in L.A., my home here on Bainbridge Island is private. It's in a remote area of the island, so I don't have neighbors who are close by, which is a plus. Also, access to the island here is limited, which is another plus, since it means that I don't have unexpected visitors just dropping in. I can always see who's coming before they get here.

I enjoy my privacy, and unlike life in even a staid tract home like I have in L.A., I have even more control. Everything is far more predictable. It's why I like coming home to Seattle to rest and recharge before I pick up my work again. It gives me a good opportunity to enjoy life in the city I was born near, and will likely die in. Hopefully, not for a while yet though.

While I don't have many fond memories of my childhood— it was terrible beyond measure— I have created my own memories. Better ones. Memories that I will be able to look back on fondly many years from now while I enjoy my golden years. Memories that will sustain me for the rest of my life.

As I think about the child in the other room and the payday that should be coming my way, my thoughts turn to the man I saw in the Morgan household today. My curiosity piqued, I go into the bedroom that I've converted into my media office and flip on the bank of eight computer screens mounted to the wall.

I sit down at the desk and type in the commands to remotely access the audio and visual equipment I'd installed in the Morgan's house by posing as the cable repairman. For somebody who just had their child abducted, you would think they'd be more careful about who they let into their house. But that is not my concern.

"Drats," I mutter to myself.

I hadn't gotten the camera into the foyer until after the mystery man had arrived, so I missed the introductions. Which means I did not get his name. I watch the conversation between them all play out though, intrigued by this man. I am relatively certain he isn't a cop. I just didn't get that feel from him, and my instincts rarely prove to be wrong.

But who is he? Some private investigator? The Morgans are filling him in on what was happening with Jordan and my ransom demands, which is interesting. And technically, since he's not a cop, I suppose they didn't break my rules. But I do plan on mentioning it.

I play and replay the video footage again and again because there is just something about him that seems... familiar. I can't say how or why, but he is definitely tickling something in my mind. It's irritating me because my memory is usually sharp, and I can recall most anything I need to when I need to remember it. But when it comes to the man in the Morgan house, I am drawing a complete blank. It's frustrating.

That is the only variable I can't account for, simply because I don't know who this man is or what role he is going to play. Perhaps it's benign. Or perhaps it's something else. I need to know which it is because I do not like having loose ends and variables I haven't factored into play.

I'm going to need to find out who this is and what he's got to do with this. I'm in control of this situation, and I don't want anybody else getting the mistaken idea that they are.

SEVEN
PAXTON

Morgan Residence; Windermere, WA

"Remember, relax and do not let him rattle you. No matter what he says," I tell Kayla. "Guys like this need to have absolute control. He will try to shake you and get under your skin. Don't let him."

She nods. "O—okay. I'll try."

We're crowded around the phone that sits on the replica Resolute Desk in Joseph's office. Subtle. The air around us is thick with the scent of lemon and wood polish. One entire wall holds a floor-to-ceiling bookcase stuffed with dozens of volumes ranging from historical biographies to the latest Michael Crichton novel. The spines all look well broken in. These books aren't just for show.

"Don't just try, Kayla," I urge. "It's critical that you

remain in control. That you show no emotion whatsoever. Guys like this feed off it."

I glance at my watch and see that it's five fifty-eight. We've got two minutes. I expect the man will make us wait five minutes or so, just to reinforce the notion that he's in control by making us wait on him. It's a cheap psychological tactic that's more annoying than it is effective. But this is his show, and if we want to get Jordan back, we have to let him play it out.

"Maybe we should have called the police after all," Joseph sighs. "Maybe they could have traced the call—"

"No, he'll kill Jordan," Kayla cries. "You heard what he said, Joseph."

Joseph looks scared. Petrified. As we get closer to the appointed hour, his fear seems to be growing while Kayla remains steadfast in her belief that she's handling this the right way. It's the first crack I've seen between them, and I need to shore it up.

"Kayla is right, Joseph," I say. "A guy like this isn't going to be able to be traced. He'll use a burner phone, and he'll destroy it right after using it."

"How many kidnappings have you worked, Mr. Arrington?" he asks.

I clear my throat. I don't know what Brody told them about our track record, but I don't get the idea that they know this is my first case as a PI. It's obviously not going to inspire a lot of confidence in them to know I'm just getting my feet wet, so I can't tell them that. But I needed to ensure they have confidence in me.

"I was Seattle PD for over nine years before becoming a private investigator. First as a cop, and then as a detective," I tell them, hoping it will instill a bit of confidence in me. "I know how criminals think. How they work. Just trust me, follow my lead, and we'll get through this together. We'll get Jordan back to you safely."

Joseph opens his mouth to reply but the phone rings, cutting him off. I glance at my watch and see that it's six o'clock straight up, which surprises me. I had expected him to make us wait. Kayla and Joseph both tense up, their faces tight with fear.

"Okay Kayla, this is it," I tell her. "Remember everything I told you. Stay calm. Be firm. Show no emotion."

She draws in a deep breath then lets it out slowly. She closes her eyes, then picks up the phone and presses it to her ear.

"H—hello," she says with only a slight flutter in her voice.

Her face twists with confusion, and she cuts her eyes to me. "Y—yes," she says. "O—okay."

Kayla reaches down and punches the button to put the call on speaker and drops the handset into the cradle.

"I would like to know who the gentleman with you is, please," the kidnapper says, his heavily modulated voice echoing around the office.

"How do you know there's somebody with us?" Joseph asks, his voice pinched with anxiety.

"That does not matter," the man says. "I would like to know who he is and why he is there. I told you, no police."

They both cut a look at me, their eyes wide, the expressions of absolute terror on their faces matching. I give them a tight smile and a nod.

"I'm not a cop," I say. "I'm here to facilitate the exchange and ensure everything goes smoothly."

"And what is your name, please?" he asks.

"Paxton Arrington," I reply. "And what is your name?"

"Paxton Arrington," he repeats. "I see."

"And your name?"

He chuckles softly. "Surely, you can't be that dim," he says. "You may call me Reuben Hayes."

The name tickles the keys of familiarity in the back of my mind, but I can't quite put my finger on it right away. But a moment later, it occurs to me. I'm hit with a wave of serendipity so powerful and deep I feel like I can't breathe for a moment. Reuben Hayes is the name of the villain in a story called The Adventure of the Priory School, written by Sir Arthur Conan Doyle. It's a Sherlock Holmes story.

In the story, Hayes is hired by a man named James Wilder to abduct the ten-year-old child of the Duke of Holdernesse, forcing him to change his will. The finer points of the story aren't entirely relevant. The fact that the man on the other end of the line has adopted the name of Reuben Hayes is. And the fact that the abductor is assuming the identity of a Holmes villain immediately makes me feel as if I am meant to be the one on this case. As if this is all some sort of kismet.

Of course, there is always the possibility that I'm overthinking this, and the abductor using the name is a simple coincidence. For all I know, it was chosen not because he somehow identifies with Hayes, or has a passion for Holmes, but because he picked two names at random. Or maybe it's the name of somebody he knows. It could be nothing more than a case of pareidolia. But it would certainly be a striking coincidence.

"Fine," I say. "I will be making the exchange tonight. So what are your instructions?"

"That is not the arrangement I—"

"If you want your money, that is the arrangement you are getting," I cut him off. "I will not risk the lives of the Morgans."

"I am a man of my word, Mr. Arrington," he says smoothly. "I have no desire to see this end in violence. This is a simple transaction."

"You'll forgive me if I choose not to take the word of a man who has kidnapped a child and is now extorting a large sum of money from her parents," I reply. "I'm sort of finicky that way."

There is a soft chuckle on the other end of the line. The eerie sound of his laughter modulated so that it sounds almost robotic, wafts through the speaker, sending chills down my spine.

"I suppose that is fair," he finally says. "And who are you to the Morgans? If I may be so bold as to ask."

"A family friend," I reply. "And somebody who cares about bringing this whole episode to a smooth, efficient, and mutually satisfactory conclusion."

There is a long pause as the man calling himself Hayes seems to be considering my words. Joseph and Kayla look at me fearfully, their eyes wide, faces drawn and pale. I give them an encouraging nod and a gesture meant to say, 'calm down'. They don't. Not one iota. And I guess, given the circumstances, I can't blame them. Also, I know I suck when it comes to being reassuring.

But what they don't know— that I fortunately do— is that this man has no desire to kill a child. I can hear it in his voice. He is cultured and refined. He is a man of learning, and for him, this transaction is all about money and nothing more. I can't explain to Kayla and Joseph how I know this. I just do. I'm as certain of it as I am my own name. They just need to trust me.

"Fine. Please use Mrs. Morgan's cell phone, so I can contact you," Hayes finally says. "In the southwest corner of Dwyer Park, there is a bridge that spans the small lake. Please be on the bridge in exactly thirty minutes. And do not be late, Mr. Arrington, I do not like to be kept waiting."

The line goes dead, and Kayla disconnects the speakerphone. They both turn to me with a million questions flashing through their eyes. And they look at me as if I have all the answers. I don't have the time to stand here and give them the answers they want, nor the reassurance they're seeking. I set the timer on my watch for thirty minutes and launch it. After he called at six o'clock on the dot, I got the impression that punctuality is very important to this man.

"Dwyer Park is fifteen minutes from here," I say. "I don't want to be late, so help me load the bags of cash."

We carry the pair of duffel bags out to my Navigator and load them into the back seat. That done, I shut the door and turn to face Kayla and Joseph, looking at each of them in the eye in turn.

"Last chance to back out of this," I say. "We can find another way."

"He'll kill Jordan," Kayla says, her brow creased with worry. "This is the only way."

"I really don't think he will," I tell them. "I don't get the sense that he would harm a child."

"What makes you say that?" Joseph asks.

I shake my head. "It's a hunch," I admit. "He just doesn't sound like a man who would kill a child to me."

Joseph and Kayla look at each other for a moment, some silent communication passing between them. And as if they've come to some telepathic agreement, then turn to me as one.

"Your instincts could be right—"

"But we aren't willing to take that chance," Kayla finishes the sentence for him. "Not with our daughter's life on the line."

I give them a nod. "Fair enough," I say. "This is your call to make."

"Do it," Joseph says. "Get our little girl back. And find out who he is if possible."

"I will," I tell them. "This will all be over soon."

As I head out, all I can hope is that this truly will be over soon and that when it is, I will be bringing Jordan home to her parents alive and well.

EIGHT

Dwyer Park; Windermere, WA

As I stand on the bridge, I can see why the man calling himself Hayes chose this spot. It's out of the way, doesn't see a lot of foot traffic at peak times, and is dark. He could be standing right beside me and I wouldn't know it until he tapped me on the shoulder.

I glance at my watch and see that thirty minutes have elapsed, and right on time, the phone in my hand rings. I connect the call.

"I'm here," I say by way of greeting.

"I can see that," he replies in his modulated robotic voice. "Thank you for being on time."

A chill, like the tip of an icy finger, slides up my spine. I have to suppress a shudder. I don't like the idea that he's out there lurking in the darkness. Able to see me, even though I can't see him. It's so dark out here in this section of the park; it tells me that Hayes has to be using night vision to see me. It's whether that night vision comes in the form of binoculars or a rifle scope that concerns me.

Just because I don't think Hayes will kill a child doesn't mean I don't think he'd kill a grown man.

What does interest me is how polite he is. The man never fails to say please and thank you. He has exceptional manners. It reinforces the notion in my mind that he is very refined, and makes me think he grew up with money, in a family where social graces mattered. It's something I can relate to. I grew up in a world where things like manners, politeness, and social graces mattered.

"How is Jordan?" I ask. "Is she safe?"

"She is in the exact same condition she was when I took her," he replies. "Not a hair out of place and not a scratch upon her skin."

It's strange to say of a kidnapper and extortionist, but I believe him. It's possible I'm entirely wrong, but I believe him when he says that Jordan is in perfect health. For some reason, my instinct that says he'd never hurt a child grows more certain.

"Why don't you come on out here and talk to me? Face to face like men," I offer.

"Nice try. But I get the feeling you're smarter than that," he replies.

"You can't blame me for trying."

"I suppose not," he says. "Where is the money, please?"

"It's close," I say. "Where is Jordan?"

"She's close," he counters. "Here is what's going to happen. You are going to go back to your car where you will remove the bags of money and leave them on the ground. You will then get in your car and drive to the location I provide. Once you arrive at said location, I will give you Jordan's location, and you can go and collect her. We both get what we want."

"I don't think so," I tell him. "You will get your money when I get the girl."

"Please do not presume, just because we are speaking amiably, that you have any sort of control or leverage here," he says. "Believe me when I say that if you do not do as I say, I will kill the girl."

"See, that's the thing. I don't think you will," I say. "You don't have it in you to kill a child. I get the impression that for you, this is purely transactional. You would rather die yourself than kill a child."

"Is that what your profile says about me?" he chuckles. "That I won't kill a child?"

"In fact, it does," I reply.

Over the last few months, even before getting fired, I did a lot of studying. Criminal psychology, FBI profiling techniques, abnormal psych... pretty much anything relating to the criminal mind. I wanted to brush up and enhance my own base of information and knowledge to better prepare me for this endeavor. I might be overeducated for a PI, but at least I'll never feel out of my intellectual depth.

"Profiles can be wrong. Profiles depend on humans and their knowledge of psychology and observation of behavioral patterns," he says. "And we both know how... unreliable... humans are. Yes?"

"You are not wrong about that. Any of it," I acknowledge. "But if you know what you're doing, more times than not, the profile you develop will be right on the money."

He chuckles. "And what does your profile tell you about me?"

"Well, that you're not a child killer."

"But what if I am a killer?"

"It's possible, and I've taken that into account," I say. "But I don't think you'd kill a child."

"And why is that?"

I shift the phone to my other ear and casually glance around, searching the darkness for some sign of him. I peer through the deep pockets of shadows, looking for movement in the gloom or perhaps a light from his phone. I search for something. Anything. But I see nothing. The man is very good and knows how to leave no visible trace of himself. He knows how to be invisible.

And that tells me this isn't his first time doing this. He's smart and savvy. He knows how to cover his tracks and take all precautions against being seen or giving himself away. He's skilled and clever. Smooth and in control of himself and the situation— and he's experienced. That is all bad news for me because it means the man does not rattle easily, and he is not the sort of man who is prone to panic or making mistakes.

"You're punctual and demand that of others. You are articulate, exceedingly polite, and seem to be well-read and well educated. And your manners and mannerisms, to me, speak to a man of stature and high class. Or at least, to a man who has learned to mimic the behaviors of those elites to the point that you believe you are one of them," I recite. "I believe that to somebody like you, immersed in that sort of social strata, harming a child would be an affront to that station. An outrageous behavior that not even you could abide."

"It is interesting that you have developed such a detailed profile in such a short period of time," he says. "And with such a limited amount of data. After all, this is only our second conversation."

"I'm a quick study."

"You should not, however, presume to believe you know everything about me."

"I would never presume such a thing," I reply.

He pauses on the other end of the line so long, I might think he'd hung up if I didn't hear the train whistling in the background of the phone as well as in my own ears. He's close. Very close. I strain my eyes again, peering into the darkness, trying to see a silhouette, a shadow moving among the shadows or anything that might give him away. But there is nothing to be seen.

"Try as you might, you will not be able to discern my location visually."

"It never hurts to be thorough," I reply.

He chuckles softly. "You are an interesting character, Mr. Arrington."

"As are you, Mr. Hayes," I say with a grin. "But tell me, will we find a Mr. James Wilder pulling your strings?"

I can all but hear the smile in his voice when he speaks. "So you know the reference. That makes you even more interesting to me," he says. "But alas, there is no Mr. Wilder behind the scenes. I am merely a man trying to secure my future."

"So of all the characters out there, why choose Hayes?" I ask. "A bit player in a bigger drama."

"Hayes is quiet. Unassuming. Not the man you would expect to find," he replies. "Also, he's obscure enough as a character that not many people would know the reference."

"I was something of a Sherlock aficionado when I was younger," I reply.

"That is an interesting fact about you," he says. "There seem to be so few of us these days."

"Indeed," I reply. "Now, about Jordan—"

"I have already told you how to retrieve her. It is now up to you to follow my instructions," he cuts me off. "While the girl is in peak health right now, if you leave her where she is too long, I cannot say that will remain the case. It is your move, Mr. Arrington."

He has the upper hand, and I know it. Even worse, he knows it. There is nothing I can do to talk him into giving Jordan up until I give him the money. If I refuse to play by his rules, she loses. Joseph and Kayla are already prepared to lose the money so long as they get their daughter back alive and unharmed. My only function here is to ensure that happens.

"Fine," I say. "We'll do this your way."

"Very good, Mr. Arrington," he says. "Little Jordan will be home, safe and sound, all snug in her bed in no time then."

He disconnects the call as I walk back to my car. Knowing he's out there watching me makes the darkness around me seem all the more oppressive. I don't fear him attacking me to take the money and then abscond with Jordan though. He gave me his word that this would all turn out all right so long as we played by his rules. And I think going back on his word would be as much of an affront to his sense of honor as hurting a child would be.

As strange as it seems, I believe this man's sense of honor is important to him. It is everything. He lives by his own code, and though it might not make a lick of sense to anybody else, to him it is everything. It is his entire sense of self.

I pull the pair of duffel bags out of my car and drop them onto the pavement of the parking lot. I turn and scan the darkness around me one more time, knowing he is out there watching me but can't see him through the shroud of night. The phone rings, so I connect the call and press it to my ear.

"It's all here," I say. "Two hundred and fifty grand."

"Please open the bags so I may see the contents."

"Not the trusting sort, are you?"

"No more so than you are."

"That's fair."

I kneel down and unzip the bags, opening them wide so he can see the bundles of cash stacked inside.

"Very good," Hayes says. "Thank you. You may rezip them now, please."

I do as he says and get to my feet again, taking a step back. "You know, the bags are kind of heavy," I say. "Do you need some help getting them into your car?"

He laughs softly. "I think I can manage, but thank you for the kind offer," he replies. "You may proceed to the corner of Twelfth and Grand, where you will await further instructions."

Knowing this is a fight I can't win and focusing on my primary goal— getting Jordan back to her parents— I climb into the Navigator and head to the designated location. It's about a ten-minute drive, and just as I'm pulling to the curb, Kayla's phone rings. I connect the call and hold the phone to my ear.

"You will find Jordan in the back seat of a blue Ford minivan in front of the art theater on Western," he says. "She, unfortunately, had to be bound and gagged to prevent any— mishaps. I also sedated her, but the effects should be wearing off in the next hour or so."

"Sounds like you thought of everything."

"In my line of work, it pays to eliminate all the risk you can."

"Is that what you call abduction and extortion? Your line of work?"

He laughs, and I shake my head. I hate the way the voice modulator makes his voice sound. It's creepy.

"No, this is merely a means to an end. Distasteful. Truthfully, I hate doing it," he replies. "But one must do what one must in the service of a higher calling."

"And what exactly is your higher calling?"

He pauses a moment and seems to be considering something before he speaks again.

"My work is of the utmost importance," he says. "And I take it very seriously."

"And what is your work exactly?"

"You are a very intelligent man, Mr. Arrington. You have very keen insights and a sharp wit about you," he says. "But do not presume you know me simply because you can work up a profile. As I mentioned, sometimes profiles are mistaken."

"Judging by the tension I hear in your voice, I'd say my profile hits pretty close to the mark," I reply. "You sound... defensive."

"Hardly," he replies. "I am intrigued, however."

"About what?"

"About you," he says.

"Is there something, in particular, you'd like to

know?" I ask. "Perhaps we can get a drink and talk about it."

"Maybe another time."

I can't explain it exactly, but I feel like I'm being drawn into Hayes' web. I'm powerfully intrigued by him as well. For whatever reason, something about him is triggering something inside of me. I really want to find and catch this man. It's not just for Jordan. She'll be home with her parents safe and sound shortly. There is just something about him that's setting off the red flags and warning bells in my head. For all his bluster about how this is only a means to an end, he's done this before. And he might do it again.

There is a lot more to this man than meets the eye. He's got many different facets to him, most of which are obscured from my sight. But the more I listen to him speak, the more small details I pick up on, the more I want to know. No, need to know. And it's because I think Hayes— or whatever his real name is— is more than just a kidnapper and extortionist. I can't say why for sure, but I am positive, beyond all reasonable doubt, that this man is a far bigger evil than he's letting on. The man on the other end of the line is a monster. A bona fide, bodies in the crawlspace under the house, heads in the refrigerator, monster.

"Before we part ways for the night," he says, "I would like you to remember three names: Kimberly Griffin, Arnold Cooper, and Jackson Wilkerson."

"And what am I supposed to do with those names?"

He laughs quietly. "I think you'll discover for yourself, once you do a little digging," he says. "You won't find a James Wilder, but you will find something else you are not expecting."

A tingle of excitement sends an army of goosebumps marching across my skin. I don't know for sure what I'm going to find once I run down those names, but something is telling me that it's going to confirm what I'm already thinking... that this man is a monster.

And it's up to me to catch him.

"Goodnight, Mr. Arrington," he says. "And I wish you all the best."

The line goes dead in my hand. I stare at it stupidly for a moment, as if expecting him to call back. He doesn't, of course. He got what he wanted and pointed me in the direction of that which I want.

I pull away from the curb and drive to the art theater. In the back of a blue minivan, I find Jordan just as he said, bound and gagged, sedated and asleep, but otherwise completely unharmed. I let out a small breath of relief. I was right about him after all.

As I drive her back to the Morgans' home, I mull the names over for a moment. None of them mean anything to me. But Hayes would not have given them to me if they didn't mean something. I suppose they mean something to him. Though I have the certainty of feeling that in time, those names will come to mean something to me as well.

Just as I have the certainty of feeling that this is not

going to be the final time I am going to hear from the man calling himself Hayes. I feel as if I'm being inexorably pulled into something much, much bigger. And far more sinister.

And as terrible as it seems, I'm excited about it.

NINE

Arrington Investigations; Downtown Seattle

"Jordan made this for you," Brody says and tosses a card down on my desk with a grin.

I pick up the colorful card made from a piece of construction paper. On the front is a giant happy face with hearts all around it and on the inside are the words, "Thank You!" in big, bold letters. It makes me smile.

"That's sweet," I say. "But it's not like I did anything. I dropped off a couple of bags and drove their daughter home. Uber could have done that."

"Don't sell yourself short. You put yourself in harm's way for Jordan," Brody says. "Kayla and Joseph aren't going to forget that."

I lean back in my chair and look at the card. The Morgans have been generous and thankful for me bringing Jordan back to them. And likely because they've been handing out my card over the past few weeks, we've gotten a steady stream of clients walking through the door. Mostly bitter men and women looking for dirt to use against their spouses in their forthcoming divorce proceedings. It's been an education.

I have spent more time camped outside of hotels than I care to admit. This is not the sort of work I'd envisioned myself doing when I hung up my shingle. I'd imagined doing more important work. But I suppose not every single case is going to be exciting. It was the same way when I was with the SPD— some calls were a rush of adrenaline, while others were routine and boring. I suppose you have to take the good with the bad.

The one thing that's stuck with me though is him. Mr. Hayes. I've tried running down the names he gave me, but as of yet, I've not come up with anything concrete. Nothing to tell me why he gave me those names, who they are, or what it means. I know it means something; otherwise, he wouldn't have given them to me. But what?

"How is she doing?" I ask. "Jordan?"

"She's good," he replies. "Kayla says the night terrors are starting to subside."

"Good. That's good."

He drops down into the chair across from me and slumps back casually. "So what's on the docket for the night?"

"I have to follow Murray Taub and get photos of him with his eighteen-year-old mistress," I groan.

"Murray Taub? The guy who owns that chain of steakhouses?"

"One and the same," I confirm.

"That guy has to be like sixty," Brody scrunches up his face in disgust. "And he's out there with high schoolers?"

"According to the soon to be ex, Mrs. Taub."

"Hey, say what you want about me, but at least I keep it strictly twenty-one and up. I can't mess around with anyone who can't at least have a drink with me. That's just nasty."

A man stands on the other side of my office door, and I wave him in. He's tall, lean, has shaggy hair, glasses, and a mustache. He's got on a red ballcap with our cable company logo on it with matching coveralls. He walks over, thrusting his aluminum clipboard at me. I take it and sign my name to the work order attached to it and hand it back.

"I think we're good to go here, Mr. Arrington," he says, tearing one of the sheets off the work order and dropping it on my desk. "Checked all the lines and computers in the office, and everything looks okay."

I nod. "Thank you."

"Happy to help," he says. "Just call us if you have any problems."

I give him a nod, and the man turns and leaves my office. Brody watches him go and turns back to me.

"I thought you were the computer guy," I say. "Why'd we have to call a repairman?"

"Just needed some networks set up. He contracts with building maintenance. Besides, I'm a computer wizard," he corrects me. "I don't do IT grunt work, but if you need the skinny on anybody, anywhere, then I'm your guy."

"Nobody says 'the skinny' anymore."

"I do."

"That's why you're single," I say. "So, any luck with those names?"

He shakes his head. "With nothing but names to go on and zero context, I don't even know what I'm looking for," he says. "And let's face it, those aren't exactly unique names. There are hundreds of people with those same names scattered around the country. Teachers, doctors, husbands, wives... no way to tell who it is this guy wants you looking at or why."

"It has to mean something," I mutter to myself.

"I think he was yanking your chain, man. I think he wanted you to do what you're doing right now— chasing your own tail trying to figure out the meaning behind all this," he says. "I bet you he pulled those names out of thin air just to make you spin your wheels."

"Actually, I wouldn't be so sure about that."

We both snap our heads up to see Blake standing in the doorway. I'd been so consumed with my thoughts I never even saw her come in.

"Hey, man," Brody says. "I'm offended. You call the

Feds to do the deep dive? What do you even have me around for?"

"Comic relief."

Brody laughs and gets to his feet. "You're a jerk," he says. "I'm going down to Starbucks. You guys want anything?"

"The usual," I say.

"I'll have what he's having," Blake adds.

"See?" I say. "This is what I keep you around for."

He gives me the finger and laughs as he leaves the office. I get to my feet and give her a hug. I open the door to my office and lead her out to the main floor, dropping down at the large conference table near the window. She takes the seat across from me, dropping her satchel on the table beside her.

"Sorry, was feeling claustrophobic in there," I say. "Good to see you, Blake."

"Good to be seen."

After Brody and I had come up empty with the names for a week straight, I'd called Blake to see if she could find anything. She's got access to state and federal databases and can do a far deeper dive than we can.

"So, I take it you found something?" I ask.

"Of course I did," she scoffs. "Did you really think I wouldn't?"

I give her a small grin. "I figured if I couldn't find it, there was nothing to be found."

"Wow, your arrogance knows no bounds," she raises an eyebrow.

"You've known me how long? This can't be news to you."

"No, I just keep hoping to humble you at some point by reminding you that you're not infallible."

I laugh. "You having better databases to work with doesn't mean I'm not infallible," I tell her. "Just so you know."

"Keep telling yourself that."

I know people think I can be arrogant. It's one of the reasons I was dismissed from the force, wasn't it? But the truth of the matter is that I have a very low tolerance for nonsense and ignorance. And I'm not afraid to call people out. Those two things have combined to give me a bad rap in some circles. Some think I'm the kind of guy who holds himself apart from others. The sort of guy who thinks I'm better than anybody, or as Deputy Chief Torres so eloquently put it, that I'm the smartest kid in the room.

Frankly, there are a million different opinions about who I am floating around out there. Everybody seems to know me better than I know myself. They all have an opinion about me. It's one reason I tend to hold myself apart from people and keep everybody at an arm's distance. They call me arrogant and aloof. I simply say I'm sick and tired of other people thinking they're entitled to have an opinion about me or tell me who they think I am. It's part of the price to be paid for growing up in the spotlight cast over the family I was raised in.

Blake knows that. She gets it and sees through the

walls I put up around myself. As do the people I deem most important to me. Everybody else, those who don't know me and I don't want to know, can beat it as far as I'm concerned.

"So what did you find?" I ask.

"I pored over data from all over the country," she says. "I started with the obvious— kidnappings. But none of the names listed were children who were kidnapped."

"I have a feeling that he does this from time to time, but it's not a real regular thing for him."

"Right. So then I started digging through homicide cases," she says. "And I found a nexus between the three names."

"You did?" I ask, honestly a little surprised.

She opens her satchel and produces three file folders with a flourish. She tosses them onto the table and grins at me. I lay them out in a line and open them one by one, quickly scanning through the police reports, but nothing in them overtly stands out to me at first blush.

"Kimberly Griffin, age twenty-nine, of Taos, New Mexico. Died of manual strangulation," Blake recites the particulars by memory.

"Prostitute," I say, reading from the report.

"Arnold Cooper, age thirty-seven, of Scottsdale, Arizona," she continues. "Died of exsanguination caused by a severing of the carotid artery."

"Construction foreman."

"And Jackson Wilkerson, age eighteen, of San

Diego, California. Died of blunt force trauma to the head," she says. "His skull was literally bashed in."

"College freshman."

I look up from the files and eye her questioningly. "I don't see the nexus."

"Look at the crime scene photos," she says. "Look at them carefully and tell me what you see."

I pull the crime scene photos for Kimberly Griffin and study it closely. She was a redhead. Pretty, if a little rough looking. Or at least, she had been in life. Her skin is pale, her eyes wide and unseeing. I turn to the construction worker and find him with that same fixed look of death on his face I've seen on more corpses than I can count in my life.

There is a clean, smooth slice across Arnold Cooper's neck and a wide pool of dark, viscous blood all around him. He'd definitely bled out. I finally turn to the college kid, and this one makes me wince. There are no discernible features left of his face. A blood-soaked baseball bat lay near the body, obviously discarded by the killer.

"Man. You weren't kidding," I say. "His skull was bashed in."

Blake says nothing. She crosses her legs and sits back in the wide, plush chair, her hands folded in her lap. She just watches me. Waiting. I examine the pictures again closely, taking in all of the details, my mind absorbing them like a sponge, and when I get to a close-up shot of the kid's body, I pause. My eyes grow wide, and my mouth falls open.

I find the close-up body shot of all three murder victims and set them all down in a line. It doesn't take me long to find what I'm looking for.

"Well, I'll be," I mutter. "Why wasn't this flagged before now?"

She shrugs. "Different states, different MO's, different jurisdictions, wasn't relevant to the murder," she says. "At least, it didn't seem to be relevant to anybody at the time."

"I'd say it's pretty relevant now."

She nods. "Yeah. To say the least."

On the inside of the left wrist on each victim is a tattoo of a cross with a flame behind it. It's small and discreet. Nothing in this day and age of people tattooing every square inch of skin on their bodies. It looks like a temporary tat, which is probably why it didn't get flagged. But as I look more closely at it, I see that there's something a little strange about it. I look up at Blake.

"Were these… painted on?"

She nods. "My best guess is a template and an airbrush or spray can for fast application."

"Jesus," I gasp.

"Pretty sure he's not involved with this," she quips.

"Probably not," I say. "Okay, so this guy is sending us a message."

"No, he's sending you a message," she replies. "He told you about these three. What's he trying to tell you?"

I look at the three summaries sitting before me, scanning the information, taking it all in, and there is one thing that stands out to me: these murders were all committed in 1998. Twenty-two years ago. If there is a message for me here, I don't see it just yet.

"He's been at this for a long time," I muse.

She nods. "A serial murderer who's been killing for two decades running."

"I don't think these were his first murders though," I say. "I have a feeling that one's special. Not one he'd share with me."

"Probably right," she says. "But why is it important to him that you know what he's been up to for the last twenty years?"

I sit back in my chair and work through the question. It doesn't take me long to hit on the answer. It seems too easy, but in my experience, the simplest answer is usually the correct one.

"He wants me to chase him," I say. "He wants to match wits with me to see if I can stop him. Those names are his challenge to me."

Blake's expression grows sober, and I see her body tense up as she looks at me. She knows I'm right. And I can tell by the expression on her face that she doesn't like it. Not one bit.

"You can't get involved with this," she says quietly. "This is dangerous, Pax. Way too dangerous for you."

"Then why did you bring me the files?"

She trails her fingernail along the grain of the

wooden table. "Mostly, I wanted to see if my own theories were right. If I was only seeing what I wanted to see, or what was really there."

"What do you mean?"

She looks up at me, and her face is strained. Pinched. She looks haunted. It's an expression I know well. After nearly ten years with the SPD, I'd seen more than a few cops who wore that same look. It's the look of a case that really got under your skin and that you could never seem to shake. It follows you everywhere. Blake is just usually so good at compartmentalizing; I never thought I would see it on her face.

"Talk to me," I tell her.

"When I started working in Seattle, I was assigned to close out a string of cold cases dating back to the early 2000s. But there were a few that stuck out to me. Five were open cases that landed on my desk because they were local. Older cases from before my time that had just never been closed. So-called disposable people. The homeless. Prostitutes. Junkies. Six, all told," she explains. "Because they were people with high-risk lifestyles, SPD did a half-assed job handling the cases and never linked them."

"But you did."

She nods. Blake slips another file out of her satchel and slides it over to me. I open it and see that it contains six crime scene photos. It doesn't take me long to spot what she wants me to see: the cross with the flame behind it at each scene.

"It's not on their skin," I say.

She shakes her head. "I think that's why the connection was never made. It was spray-painted on walls or dumpsters. But always near the body," she says. "So when I saw the tats on the wrists of the murder vics he gave you, the connection was instant."

It was instant because those first six cases are never far from her mind. She's held onto them all these years.

"Why did these stick with you?" I ask.

Her smile is tight, her face drawn. "The first vic I found personally was a fifteen-year-old girl. Prostitute," she tells me. "Teresa Reyes. She was just so young and…"

Her voice trails off, but she doesn't need to finish the statement. I get it. I can see the emotion swirling in her eyes and can see just how hard this is all hitting her. It's like ripping open an old wound. But true to form, the ever-stoic Blake is holding it all in, refusing to let her emotions run roughshod over her. I watch as she stuffs it all down deep inside then turns her cool green eyes on me.

"You never told me any of this," I note.

"It's not exactly the sort of thing you bring up at dinner parties," she admits. "Besides, this one was personal. I vowed that eventually, I'd find the man who did it."

"Why didn't anybody look into it after you found the link?"

"Nobody wanted to touch it. These kinds of cases

aren't high up on the priority list. You know how that goes," she spits, her bitterness apparent. "My supervisor said it was flimsy at best. Said the crosses were probably just graffiti, and anyway, it had long since been cleaned up. Refused to let me work them. Declared it a waste of time, since not even the SPD was looking into it."

I shake my head. "Yeah, that figures."

"Anyway, with nine confirmed victims, we're chasing a dangerous guy, Pax. A really dangerous guy," she says. "I don't want you involved. I don't want you anywhere near this."

"It's too late," I tell her. "I'm already involved. Like you said, his message was for me."

"Let us handle it," she argues. "Seriously, this is getting serious. We'll take it from here."

"You think your bosses are going to let you run with this? They didn't before, Blake," I contest. "And because of that, this guy has been running around butchering people for the last twenty years."

"But now we've got new information. Definitive links. I've also got more seniority and clout now," she says. "They'll have to let me open a book on this."

This is as close to bigfooting her way onto a case as I've ever seen her come. But I know it's because she's afraid for me. I know she doesn't want anything to happen to me any more than I want anything happening to her. And when you have a serial killer who has been operating for at least twenty years, you have to assume that not only is he cagey and intelligent, but dangerous.

But more than that, I can see how personal this is for her. I can see how badly she wants to catch this guy. I would have a better chance of stopping the sun from rising tomorrow than I do of getting Blake to back off of this. Now that we have a link and a lead, she's going to go full bore on it.

"I can't stop you from taking this back to headquarters," I say. "But you can't stop me from looking into this on my own. And I think if we pool our resources, we'll stand a much better chance of getting this guy."

"Pax, this isn't a game," she says, sitting up, a hard edge in her voice. "This man has been killing for twenty years. And now he wants to draw you into his game."

"I can take care of myself."

"Shut up," she snaps. "This is not the time to go all alpha male on me. This is serious."

"I know it is. I know this isn't a game," I say. "But nobody's gotten a sniff of this guy for two decades. Until now. I have a chance to—"

"This isn't about you, Pax!" she roars, jumping to her feet. "This isn't about feeding your ego."

"I disagree. He made it about me."

"Don't be stubborn. Stay out of this," she says. "I'm begging you."

I look at her for a long moment, and she sits back down, letting out a long breath as if to calm and gather herself. She knows she can't stop me from doing this.

"It's like I told you, Blake. I got into this because I want to make a difference," I tell her. "I want to do some good, some actual good, in this world. I guarantee Veronica would have told me to see this through."

She laughs softly and shakes her head, looking down at her hands. Her concern is well-intentioned. It's not like I don't appreciate her looking out for me. I absolutely do. She's a good friend like that. But this is something I feel like I have to do. I feel it down deep in my bones. Veronica would absolutely want me to chase this guy down.

"If I can help catch somebody who's been killing for two decades, I'd say that's doing a little bit of good in the world," I say. "I'd say it's helping keep Veronica's spirit alive."

She arches an eyebrow, a crooked grin pulling a corner of her mouth upward. "You're a jerk to play the dead wife card," she says. "You know that, don't you?"

"According to you, I'm a jerk anyway."

"That's true," she replies. "But playing the dead wife card makes you more of a jerk."

I flash her a grin and look down at the photos on my desk again. My eyes are drawn to the temporary tattoos the man placed on the victims and think about what they might mean to him. Judgement, perhaps? Salvation? Does he believe he's saving their souls? Cleansing the world?

"I know I can't stop you from looking into this. Mostly because you're a stubborn jerk," she sighs. "But I want you to keep me in the loop every step of the way."

"Deal."

"And also, if it starts getting too hairy if things look like they could go sideways, pull the plug and walk away," she orders. "I'm serious, Pax. Don't put yourself in any danger. If you can promise me those things, I'll do anything I can to help. Run down names, backgrounds—anything."

"I promise." I flash her a grin. "And when I catch this guy, I'll even let you make the arrest. It'll look good for your career. I'm magnanimous like that."

She laughs softly but doesn't say anything more. I can tell she's worried. Blake thinks I'm too rash sometimes and do things without thinking. She's not entirely wrong, but I am also far more deliberate than she gives me credit for. I take time to think about the situation. It's just that I can process my thoughts and form a plan of action faster than most people, so it simply looks like I'm being rash and foolhardy. Most of the time, anyway.

But Blake worries for me, and I don't discount that. I appreciate her concern. She knows that she can't stop me from doing this. But by giving me the green light, I can see she now feels responsible for me. She looks down at her hands again for a moment, doing her best to control the maelstrom of emotions I see churning across her face. But rather than continue her lecture, she surprises me when she stands up suddenly.

"I need to get back to the office," she says. "I've got some work to do to get the ball rolling on this."

I get up and walk her through the office, pausing just outside the elevator doors. She turns to me, and though she's wearing a smile, I can see the turbulent emotions churning behind her eyes. She's not thrilled with this arrangement. But I can also see excitement mixed in with it all. The thrill of the chase. I get that too.

I arch an eyebrow at her. "If I was still a detective, you wouldn't be this worried."

"Of course I would be. But you're not a detective anymore; you're a civilian," she retorts. "And as far as I know, you don't even have a weapon to defend yourself with."

"Being a civilian allows me to go places detectives can't go. Do things detectives can't do," I point out. "And I've already got my application in for a concealed carry permit. I won't be defenseless."

She sighs and shakes her head. "I guess you've thought of everything."

"Don't I always?"

Blake laughs softly and punches me in the shoulder. "Well, Sherlock, it looks like you've found your Moriarty."

I flash her a wolfish grin in return. "And the game is afoot."

"The game's been afoot for twenty years, dummy."

I shrug. "Yeah well, it sounded cool to say."

"It really didn't."

TEN

REUBEN HAYES

Bainbridge Island, WA

Paxton Arrington. The eldest son of Harvey and Jessica Arrington, Harvey being the current CEO of Archton Media, and Jessica being a socialite and philanthropist. These people are old money, and their family built their empire from the ground up, with each successive generation adding to that empire. I have to respect that.

And from everything I've read, Paxton and his siblings aren't the sort of silver-spooned trust fund babies you see in some tabloid scandal every week. No, they were expected to work. To earn their place. Sure, they obviously have advantages that most of us don't— that I certainly never had growing up— but according to everything I've found, the Arringtons don't just hand the reins over to the next in line just because. They have to prove themselves and earn it. I have to respect that too.

I sit back and study the bank of monitors on the wall before me. I am learning everything there is to know about Paxton Arrington— 'Pax' to his friends, which I find especially loathsome. I must say, he has quite an interesting story. The eldest son and presumptive heir to the media empire his family began generations ago, who spurned that life for a life of service. He joined the police force at age twenty-four and served the city of Seattle first as a beat cop, then as a detective, until his dismissal four months ago at the age of thirty-four.

In between, he got married, then became a widower a few short years later. His late wife, Veronica, had an interesting story of her own. But she's not relevant to what's happening right now, so I don't need to learn everything about her. I only need to know where her life intersects with Paxton's. And I see it's there, where they met when young Paxton began to change.

It's clear to me his wife had some kind of earth-shattering impact on him because he went from blueblood and a media mogul in waiting, to beat cop, then SPD detective, and now PI. He shifted from a life of privilege and luxury to one of the most thankless, difficult professions imaginable. It's something you don't see very often, which makes him especially interesting to me. And it makes me see just how big of an impact Veronica must have had on him.

As I watch the monitors, I see a tall woman with

strawberry blonde hair step off the elevator and enter the office suite. I'd managed to get my cameras and audio equipment into the main part of the office suite earlier using the same ruse as at the Morgans' house. I monitored the building's communications long enough to wait for them to need maintenance on his floor, then disguised myself as a contractor to slip in unnoticed.

It's disturbing how many people don't pay attention to who they're letting into their lives. But it suits my purposes just fine.

Eventually, I will need to find a way to get my equipment into Paxton's personal office as well as that of his partner. This will do for now, though. I watch her in Paxton's office from the camera hidden in the lobby and wish I could hear what they're saying to one another. But then Paxton's partner leaves the office, and he leads the mystery woman out to a table in the open space on the floor. Perfect.

"And who are you?" I wonder aloud as I look at the woman.

I watch them interact for a bit. They figured out the three names I gave to Paxton the night of the ransom drop. It was the mystery woman who cracked the code on that particular clue, which I find somewhat disappointing since I've got such high hopes for Paxton.

There are very few people who would know the name Reuben Hayes so quickly. He's such an obscure character in a book that has gone well out of style these days. Nobody reads the classics anymore. That Paxton knew the name off the top of his head like that sent a charge through me. Something I haven't felt in a very long time.

I watch the body language of the two and listen to their conversation. She's a very clever woman to have found out my clues so quickly. From their conversation, I glean that she is experienced at this and has access to classified databases. Possibly a federal agent. She could very well be as intellectually formidable as Paxton. And with her in his corner, it means I will need to up my game even higher. Which is good, I like a challenge, and it seems ages since I've had a genuine one.

I am excellent at reading body language, and as I watch the pair, it seems to me they're very close, and there's a genuine affection between them. I don't get the sense that it's romantic, though. It seems like it's a mutual respect, admiration, and a deep friendship, more than anything.

"Enter Irene Adler," I muse. "Or perhaps you, and not his business partner, are his Watson."

A smile touches my lips as I watch them flipping through the files Ms. Adler brought along with her. We're off to a good start. They have identified my first three victims— or at least, the first three victims I'm giving them. My victims prior to those three, do not count since they were not part of my work. I consider them to be the experimentation. Perhaps a better way to put it would be that they were a pupal phase of my becoming. Through them, I underwent a metamorphosis.

When I emerged from that chrysalis, my purpose was clear. I've never been a particularly religious man. I've seen firsthand just how destructive and immoral religion can be when wielded by those who use it for their own ends. I've seen just how immoral those who claim to have faith can be. This world of ours is infested with those of low character, religious and non-religious alike. Liars, killers, rapists, cheats, and thieves. This world we live in has been overrun and is controlled by the immoral. By the corrupt.

And I, for one, have grown tired of it.

That is why I do what I do: to help cleanse this cesspool of a world we live in. I know I am but one man, but my hope is that others will follow my example and take the steps necessary to help make the world a better place. To make the world more ethical. To populate it with people of higher character and principles. I do my work to show the world that having morals is something worth striving for.

I know that in the end, my work will only amount to a drop in the bucket. But if others see what I do, take inspiration from it, and pick up the mantle of my work, maybe this world can, one day, become a place worth living in. Maybe one day, it can cease being the festering cesspool of immorality and degradation that it is right now.

That is my hope, anyway. That is why I do the

things I do.

Once upon a time, I had a normal life. I had a job. I paid my taxes. I had friends. I did all of those things normal people do. Or at least, the things society expects the so-called normal people to do. And for a time, I made myself believe that it was enough for me.

But in truth, the veneer of normalcy never fit right. It was like wearing clothing that was several sizes too small. No matter how I twisted, turned, and tried to cram myself into it, that life never fit me quite right. I was always uncomfortable. I always feared that eventually, the people in my life would see through the facade I had surrounded myself with. I worried that they would eventually stumble onto the fact that I feigned my happiness and contentment with my life because that would lead to questions I did not have the answers to. Questions I wanted to avoid altogether.

But that all changed that one fateful October night. That night started my becoming. It began my metamorphosis. It changed my life. And in my own small way, it is allowing me to change the world.

I look back up at the screen and hear Paxton uttering one of the most iconic lines in Sherlock Holmes canon. It makes me smile and deepens my feeling of serendipity.

"The game is indeed afoot, Mr. Arrington."

Ultimately, I'm going to have to kill Paxton. In my line of work, I take no risks. But in the meantime, he'll be an appropriate challenge to play with for a while.

ELEVEN

Arrington Investigations; Downtown Seattle

"You realize this is, like, totally illegal, right?"

I nod. "I do."

"I mean, we're talking don't drop the soap, multiple life sentences, federal prison illegal," Brody continues. "You get that, yeah?"

I laugh. "I'm pretty sure you don't get multiple life sentences for computer hacking."

"You could."

"Depends on the hack and the damage you do," I offer. "We aren't doing any damage."

"What we did— what you made me do— is a pretty big freaking hack, Pax."

Brody sits in the chair in front of my desk, bouncing his leg and chewing on his thumbnail, which he only does when he's extremely agitated and nervous.

"The government doesn't screw around with stuff like this, man," he sighs. "They could like, declare me a terrorist and ship me off to Gitmo or something."

I laugh. "Relax, Brody. Take a Xanax or twelve," I say. "They'll never even notice we're here."

"And how do you know that?"

"Because there's nobody I trust more when it comes to all things tech than you," I tell him. "Your hacking skills are top-notch, and because your butt was on the line, I know you took twice as much care with it."

"Cute," he sneers. "Real cute."

I lean back in my chair and laugh. "I'm only half kidding."

He drops his head into his hands. "Christ, you're the biggest dick in the world."

"Oh, I wouldn't say the biggest in the *world*. But in the Puget Sound? Yeah, probably."

We fall silent for a minute as I give Brody a minute to gather himself. He's near hyperventilating. And I get it. What I asked him to do is risky. If he gets caught, he could be in serious trouble. Not that the lawyers our families have on retainer would let anything happen to him, but I'm sure getting arrested and hauled in would be pretty intense nonetheless.

But when it comes to computers, I don't know anybody better than Brody. He's like Bill Gates level computer savvy. The things he can do are scary. There is literally nobody I would have trusted more to get me into the databases I needed access to. He hacked into and built back doors into VICAP, the NCIC, and a couple of other smaller federal criminal databases that will allow me to collect and compare as much information as possible.

Going after Reuben Hayes is going to require patience and extreme attention to detail. It will also require that I have as much data at my disposal as I can possibly have. He gave me the first breadcrumb and is clearly expecting me to follow his trail. That, of course, leads to a lot of questions I don't have the answers to, the most pertinent being: why?

Why would Hayes, who had been operating in complete anonymity for over two decades, risk it all by giving me these three victims? It makes no real sense to me. But it's also a question I don't need the answer to right this minute. It is a distraction. The important thing is, he gave them to me and invited me into his warped and twisted game. And I'm more than ready to play.

"I've never hacked a federal database," Brody says slyly, interrupting my thoughts.

I give him a grin. "Be honest. You kinda got a rush out of it, didn't you?"

A sly smile pulls the corners of his mouth up. "Yeah," he says. His expression quickly sobers. "But I'm serious man; this is something we probably shouldn't be messing around with."

"I need access to the databases without Blake knowing about it," I say. "And I swear to you that I will not let you get hit by the blowback if there is any. I will take all the heat. Your name will not pass my lips."

"Like they'll believe you hacked into their systems," he rolls his eyes. "You can barely get your electric toothbrush to work."

"I got your back," I tell him. "I mean it, dude."

He laughs nervously as I pick up the bottle of water on my desk, twist off the cap, and take a long swallow. Now that I have access to the databases I need, I can start digging up whatever dirt I need to hunt this man down. And I will hunt him down. I am going to get this guy as much for my own satisfaction and Veronica's memory as for Blake. Maybe if I take this guy down, she can finally find some peace and lay her old ghosts to rest once and for all.

"I don't feel great about this," Brody says.

"You're helping to catch a serial killer," I tell him. "So far, he's racked up nine bodies that we know of. He's been killing for twenty years. If we take him down, what's not to feel good about?"

"The whole, the Feds kicking down our door and dragging us away for hacking their database thing?"

"Relax. They'll never know we're in," I say. "And if they do, like I said, I got your back."

"All right, man. I'll take you at your word."

"It's always been good enough for you before."

"Yeah, but you never asked me to commit multiple felonies before," he replies grimly.

"Huh. I could have sworn I had," I chuckle but then

hold his gaze for a long moment. "This is for a good cause, Brody. We're doing a good thing. Just... trust me."

He grins and shakes his head. "I do, man. That's why I did it," he says. "You need anything else?"

"Yeah actually," I nod. "If you could build me a back door into the NSA..."

He bursts into laughter. "Screw you, man."

He turns and leaves my office, leaving me to my work. I've never used these databases before, and honestly, I could use Blake's help. But she would crap an absolute and probably literal brick if she knew I'd had Brody build me back doors into federal databases. About all I can do is give myself a crash course tutorial, so I settle in to do just that.

I walk out to the kitchen area and put on a pot of coffee. I have a feeling this is going to be a long night.

TWELVE

Arrington Investigations; Downtown Seattle

"You look like crap."

My eyes fly open, and a jolt of adrenaline surges through my body at the sound of her voice. I sit up and immediately regret the decision as a white-hot bolt of pain races up my back. I see Blake sitting in the chair across from me, her feet up on my desk, crossed at the ankles, and a sly smirk on her face.

"Christ, Blake," I croak. "How long have you been sitting there?"

"A while," she replies. "I would have let you sleep longer, but your snoring got to be a bit much for me."

"Bite me," I laugh.

I get to my feet and groan as I stretch my back, trying to work all of the stiffness out of my body.

"Judging by those wrinkled clothes and the drool

puddle on your desk, I'm guessing you were here all night," Blake notes.

I cut a quick glance at my desk but see no drool puddle, which makes me roll my eyes as Blake bursts into laughter.

"I see the FBI is still employing the brightest minds around," I crack.

"The best and brightest."

"Yeah, keep telling yourself that."

She picks up a bag from the seat next to her and tosses it to me. I open it up to find a ham, cheese, and spinach croissant that smells absolutely delightful. My stomach rumbles, reminding me I forgot to eat last night. I pull it out and drop the bag into my trash can, then take a big bite of it, making a noise that sounds obscene.

"You are a godsend," I mumble around a mouthful of food.

"Of course I am," she replies. "Seriously, why did you sleep at your desk last night?"

"I was tired."

"Tired of?"

"Silly questions," I say, taking another bite.

As I chew, I try to figure out how best to tell Blake what I've found. I don't want to come right out and admit that I've been using federal databases, but at the same time, she has to know what I uncovered. I promised her I'd loop her in, and this is huge.

She throws a balled-up napkin at me. "Don't be a

jerk," she grins. "You avoiding somebody? Hiding from the mob? What?"

I choke down the last of my croissant and wash it down with a bottle of room temperature water. Better than nothing. I clear my throat, sitting back and staring at her for a long moment. How can I find the right words to tell her without her blowing up at me? An uncomfortable silence passes. I can't stall on this forever. The more I think about it, the more I think it's inevitable. I have to tell her

"So, I spent the night doing some digging. Like a really deep dive into our guy," I start.

"How do you even know where to look?" she interrupts. "All we have are three vics."

"Nine. But the three he gave me seem different than the six you showed me," I go on. "They're not nearly so practiced or polished. He honed his method with these three and was ready to take the next step in his evolution."

"Okay, that's great. But you're still not answering my question," she says.

"I looked into the background of the three he gave us. Like I said, I did a deep dive," I tell her. "We have the prostitute, of course. From what I could find, she had some connections to a trafficking operation that got busted shortly after her murder. I bet she was a recruiter of sorts. The construction worker was a convicted sex offender. Child predator, to be specific. And the college kid was a dealer. Sold meth to high school-aged kids."

"Where'd you get all this?"

"I'm good at what I do," I tell her.

I hadn't needed the federal databases for all of that. Those were bits and pieces I'd discovered through more traditional means, like public records, court transcripts, and whatnot. The construction worker had been convicted and served eight years for exposing himself to a child in a public park. The college kid had a run-in with campus police for cooking meth in his dorm, but his folks covered it over with a hefty donation. No formal charges were ever filed, but he was put on campus probation.

All of that was good information and provided me with a little bit of context for the killings. The man obviously sees himself as a cleaner. Given the combination of the flaming cross iconography, I have to think he's motivated by religion. Perhaps he sees himself as an avenging angel, tasked with cleansing the world of sin. Or, it's possible religion is just an affectation, and he is simply a morally stringent man who sees evil in the sins of others.

That's all just fine details though. The most salient conclusion I've drawn is that he's a mission-oriented killer, and his mission is to rid the world of immorality. Or at least, what he decides is immorality. I feel comfortable making that determination because of what I found in my all night database binge session.

"He's preaching to us," I tell her.

"Like he's on a mission from God kind of preaching?"

I shrug. "I personally think the religious angle is just window dressing. He's a cleaner. Thinks he's cleansing the world of sin," I tell her. "He derives his moral righteousness either from God or some other higher power. Or it could just be something inside his own twisted mind that compels him."

"What aren't you telling me?" she asks, leveling an inquisitive gaze on me.

There are very few people in this world who can read me. I do my best to keep my thoughts and feelings to myself, usually wearing a carefully crafted mask of neutrality— or indifference, depending on who you ask. But Blake is one of those people who can see through it. It was the same with Veronica. She'd cut through my crap the first day we met, and that was when I knew I needed to be with her.

"I'm not sure that I should tell you," I say.

"That means you definitely need to tell me."

I laugh. "How do you figure?"

"Because if you're holding out on me, it means you've got something good," she insists. "Now, what is it? Give it up."

"Promise you won't get mad?"

"No. Of course not," she scoffs. "Because I know if you have something good enough for you to do this song and dance with me, you probably did something shady to get it."

I can't keep the smile off my face or stop the laughter from trickling out. It's funny that she knows me this well. It's also somewhat discomforting. But really if there's somebody, aside from Brody, I want to know me inside and out this way, it would be Blake. But that doesn't mean I don't need to be careful with what I say and do around her— she is still a Fed, after all. And she takes her duty very seriously.

"Let's just say in addition to the three he gave me, along with your six; I think I've identified twenty-seven other potential victims," I tell her. "Which brings our grand total of victims to thirty-six."

Her eyes widen, and her mouth falls open. Blake is silent for a long moment, seemingly too stunned to speak. I felt the same way. There may be more out there. In fact, there probably are more out there than I've been able to find. But after I got comfortable navigating the databases, I was able to hone in on some specifics, and when I finally called it quits, I had gotten a total of thirty-six murder victims that had that flaming cross either on their skin, or painted at the crime scene.

"I honestly don't know how nobody picked up on this," I tell her. "This is a colossal mess, Blake."

"Thirty-six," she gasps. "How in the..."

Her voice trails off as she continues trying to wrap her mind around the enormity of what we're dealing with. I mean, we are talking about one of the more prolific serial killers in the country's history, and he's gone undetected, cutting a bloody swath from one side of the nation to the other, for more than two decades. It's unreal and represents one of the biggest failures in law enforcement I've ever heard of.

Blake gives herself a small shake and gathers her wits about her again. She narrows her eyes and levels a suspicious gaze on me. Here it comes. I can see an eruption the size of Krakatoa looming on the not too distant horizon. But this is bigger than me. It's more important to get justice for the dead but to also bring in the killer than to worry about having Blake scream at me.

"How did you find these victims?" she asks.

I rub my chin, and the stubble makes a dry, scratchy sound. "I did some digging."

"How, Pax?" she demands, her voice carrying a hard edge to it. "How were you able to identify thirty-six victims?"

"I knew what to look for?" I reply with a grin. "If you hadn't shown me the flaming cross—"

"Cut it out, Pax. How did you do this? How did you find these victims?" she hisses. "And if you tell me it's because you're good at what you do, I swear to God; I'll kick you in the balls so hard, they'll have to remove them from your throat."

"Wow," I note. "In this era of heightened attention to police brutality, you—"

"Pax!"

Okay, I've pushed her too far. Clearly. If looks could kill, I would be dead ten times over right now. There's no sense in putting it off any longer. It's not like she's going to suddenly forget. I have a feeling the next step is going to be a blowtorch and pliers to get the information out of me if I don't tell her.

"I was poking around a few databases and—"

"What databases?" she snaps.

I purse my lips then try to give her the most charming smile I can muster. It doesn't work. She narrows her eyes further and glares at me.

"Which databases, Pax?"

I sigh. "VICAP and the NCIC, primarily."

She runs a hand across her face and shakes her head. She doesn't look surprised though. Nor does she immediately go off like Vesuvius, which I find surprising. But then, maybe she's just working up to it and is going to unleash the mother of all eruptions once she's got a good head of steam up.

"How'd you get access to the databases?" she asks.

"I hacked the system."

"Brody," she groans. "I should have known."

"What? I did—"

"Please. You can barely work your phone," she cuts me off. "You actually think I believe you can hack something as complex as a federal database?"

"Let's just leave Brody out of this, all right?" I ask.

"What do you think you're doing, Pax?" she asks. "I mean, hacking a federal database? Have you lost your freaking mind?"

"I'm trying to find a killer," I fire back. "And to do that, I need every tool at my disposal."

"Yeah well, those databases weren't at your disposal."

"Until they were."

A flash of irritation crosses Blake's face. "I'm not screwing around," she says. "You could be in some serious trouble."

"Don't worry. I've got very expensive lawyers on retainer."

She blows out an exasperated breath. "Do you take anything seriously?"

I give her an even look. "I take bringing a murderer to justice very seriously," I say. "That's why I did what I did."

She opens her mouth, probably to chastise me further, but closes it again. Maybe she realizes I'm right. Or at least, she's come to see that like me, she needs every tool available to her. Which makes me a tool.

"You need to be careful, Pax," she says. "If they find out—"

"They won't," I say. "And it's not like I'm stealing information. I'm simply running some searches."

Blake rakes her fingers across her scalp and slides her fingers through her hair. I can see how frustrated she is with me, but I can also see that light of excitement in her eyes about having some new leads we can follow. It's something I can relate to.

"What have you found?" she asks.

I glance pointedly at my watch. "Wow. The reading of the riot act took less than five minutes—"

"Don't push me, Arrington," she growls. "I can still kick your nuts up into your throat, you know. I suggest you quit while you're ahead."

I hold my hands up in surrender. "Fair enough," I say. "As for what I've found like I said, thirty-six total possible vics. I spotted that flaming cross at all of the scenes, or on the vics. Discreet, as usual."

"How many states are we talking about here?"

"As far as I can tell, the vast majority of his kills have been in the western states of Washington, Oregon, and California. He's had a few in Arizona, New Mexico, and Idaho as well," I explain. "But bear in mind, there could be more out there. More that I haven't found yet."

"How did you ID these ones?"

"I ran a search," I shrug. "Given that the vics we knew of were all traffickers or dealers or predators, I narrowed it down to those types of cases or anything our perp might think of as 'sinful'. Ran checks for tattoos of flaming crosses or the presence of graffiti at the site. Had to filter out a bunch by hand. Why do you think I slept in the office?"

Blake chuckles and shakes her head. "Christ," she mutters. "Why aren't you working for the Bureau again?"

"I have a soul."

"Shut up, Arrington."

The databases themselves are basically just giant warehouses of digital information that store all the facts and figures of any given crime scene across the country.

You can plug in keywords that allow you to view the reports and photos of a wide range of crimes. It's a useful tool if you know what you're looking for. But if you don't know, then you might as well be beating your head against the wall.

The database is only as good as the information a user has. Like the old saying goes, garbage in, garbage out. For instance, if you don't know you should be combing the database for crime scenes where a flaming cross was found, guess what? You're not going to find crime scenes with flaming cross graffiti or tattoos. But knowing what we were looking for changed everything.

"This is why it's good that we're pooling our resources," I tell her. "I think of things you don't, and you sit there and look pretty."

"I've got a gun, you know."

I laugh. "The thing that's bothering me, though, is that we wouldn't be here right now without Hayes," I tell her. "He gave us the first breadcrumb we needed to find the trail."

"Which makes me wonder why," Blake adds.

"Yeah, that's something I've been wrestling with."

"He wants you to play his game for some reason," she tells me. "Which I find more than a little troubling."

"I think it's because we both share a fascination with Sherlock Holmes."

Blake rolls her eyes. "Great. Bonding with a serial killer over ancient literature."

"Well, at least you know it's literature," I say. "Good for you."

"Shut it, Arrington."

I brush her off. "It's the only thing that makes sense to me. I mean, he seemed to really perk up when I figured his alias out."

"Wonderful."

"It's not much, but it's something we might be able to use later."

"Yeah, maybe."

I scrub my face with my hands and roll my head around, trying to work out a kink in my neck. I can't get it out, and it's irritating me.

"What does your boss say?" I ask.

"I have a feeling they're going to say a lot more once they get a load of this," she tells me. "Listen, this changes things—"

"It changes nothing, Blake. It just means he's killed more people than we thought," I insist. "And it certainly doesn't change what I'm doing. Or what I'm going to do."

Blake sits up and puts her feet on the floor then starts picking imaginary lint off her slacks. She frowns.

"Figured you'd say that," she says.

"You know me well."

She stands up and looks at me, her expression sober. "Watch your six, Arrington. I'm not screwing around. This is as serious as you're going to get."

"Consider it watched."

THIRTEEN

Downtown Seattle

I stand in the alley looking up one way and down the other. There are half a dozen dumpsters; three against one wall, three against the other. Trash is piled up against the wall like snowdrifts, and the pervasive smell of decay, rotting meat, and something even more pungent that I can't identify underneath it all saturates the air. Overhead, the sky is slate gray. A fine mist drifts down from above. The cool breeze blowing down the alley carries the whispered promise of rain along with it.

The fact that the Bureau hasn't officially given Blake the green light to investigate this case is baffling. It's pissing Blake off to no end. I have to think that somebody realized they screwed up somewhere along the line and have allowed this guy to kill with impunity for decades, and now they're trying to avoid all responsibility and the scandal that will come along with it. If they don't acknowledge it, they don't have to take the blame for it.

I guess the Bureau has taken so many body blows lately, they want to step back and take a minute to catch their breath. Given what they're dealing with on their end, I suppose I can't really blame them; they really are eating crow right now and taking fire from all directions.

I check the address from the police report and double-check my location. I'm in the right spot. This is where Teresa Reyes' body was found. It's an alleyway between a Chinese restaurant and a dive bar, though I have no idea what these two businesses were ten years ago.

I don't even know what I'm doing here, honestly. It's been so long; I know there isn't going to be anything in the way of evidence to be found here. Not even the flaming cross that had been spray painted on the wall near the body remains. I guess I just want to be in the spot Blake found the body. I thought soaking in the atmosphere might give me an idea of where to go and what do to next because, at the moment, I'm coming up empty.

I'm not a trained investigator, so I'm flying by the seat of my pants right now. I'm moving by instinct. They say that if you don't get a lead within the first forty-eight hours of a murder, your chances of actually catching the suspect diminish with every passing hour. Which means that, given the fact that Teresa's murder happened a decade ago, my odds of catching the killer should be somewhere around zero.

But the killer, Hayes, put us on this path himself. He gave me the first three names and had to know that eventually, we'd make the connection to his other victims. So was this all part of his plan? Did he want us to find these other six? Did he expect us to find that Teresa Reyes was one of his? Did he expect that I would find the link to his dozens of other victims? If Blake is right and he sees himself as my Moriarty, is this all part of a test? Part of his 'Great Game'?

I hate to say it because I know how perverse and morbid it sounds, but being on the hunt for Hayes, for this most prolific of serial killers, sends a rush of adrenaline through me I haven't felt in a very long time. The man is intelligent, articulate, calculating— and ruthless. Crossing swords with him is an unexpected treat that has me vibrating with excitement.

I turn in a circle, taking in my surroundings— while doing my best to not gag on the stench— and try to visualize what it had been like that night. The ME's report said Teresa had been butchered. Thirty-one stab wounds to her chest and stomach, but the fatal blow was an ear to ear slice across the neck that severed her carotid. The savagery of the attack tells me it was personal.

Given that Teresa was a prostitute, the lazy conclusion to draw is that an angry john carved her up, which is, in fact, the conclusion the SPD came to. Given the laziness and arrogance, I now know is at all levels of the SPD, that isn't all that surprising. I don't see this man soliciting prostitutes in dark alleys though. I can't explain it, but I think he would consider it... dirty. He'd see it as being beneath him. As a ruse? Yeah, absolutely. As a means of actual sexual gratification? Probably not.

There's obviously much more to this case than that, but the detective assigned to the case— a Detective Garvin— didn't dig much deeper than the surface. Granted, the painted cross looks like graffiti in the crime scene photos, but he should have been diligent and tried to run it through the federal database just in case. But like I said, garbage in, garbage out.

I pull the crime scene photo out of the folder and walk over to the spot where Teresa's body was found. I try to picture it. I close my eyes and see the man bringing Teresa into the alley under the guise of being a client. He turns her around, makes her put her hands against the wall, and then, instead of using her, he grabs her by the hair, pulls her head back, and cuts her throat. Then, while she's gasping as her life's blood flows from the wound in her neck, the killer turns her around and stabs her over and over again.

He'd probably cut her throat first to keep her quiet. And as I look around the alley and see how much my vision is obscured by the dumpsters, fire escapes, and other assorted refuse, I see that this is an ideal spot. In the dark, it would be hard to see somebody down here, and if somebody did see him, it would be in silhouette only. And given the reputation of the neighborhood, they would probably assume he was back here being serviced by one of the prostitutes that work the area. It's just about the most perfect place to commit an evil act like what had been done to Teresa.

I slip the photo back into the file as my phone rings. I slip the file into my satchel and pull my phone out. I'm still studying the area and don't check the caller ID before I connect the call and press the phone to my ear.

"Arrington," I say.

"Mr. Arrington," he says. "It's nice to hear your voice again."

I feel like my veins have been filled with ice. My gut churns wildly with trepidation and excitement. A hot shot of adrenaline courses straight through me. It's morbid, I know, but I can't keep the small smile off my face.

"Mr. Hayes," I reply. "How did you get this number?"

"Please. You of all people know how easy it is to obtain information others don't want you to have."

His comment takes me off guard. He's clearly alluding to something, but I don't know what it is offhand. It's curious, but a nugget of information I'll store away, for now, to study later when I've got time and I'm not distracted.

"I have to admit that I'm surprised you'd contact me," I state.

"Oh? And why is that?" he asks. "I thought our last conversation went well enough, and we ended it on a positive note. You did get the girl home, after all."

"I did," I say. "You are a man of your word."

"I am at that."

I walk out of the alley just to get out of the stink and lean against the wall of the Chinese restaurant. I glance through the window and see that it's half-filled with happy patrons all stuffing their faces with noodles, rice, and a hundred other dishes I can see. If it weren't for me still feeling nauseous after being in the fetid stink of that alley for so long, I might be hungry. But at the moment, I think crackers and water is all I'll be able to tolerate.

I turn away from the window, lean my head back against the brick wall, and look up at the sky. The mist has all but stopped, but it feels like a storm is coming. I expect it to get a whole lot colder and a whole lot wetter by morning. But for the moment, I'm content to stand here and suck in lungful after lungful of clean, fresh air.

That's when it hits me that Hayes isn't using his voice modulator. He's allowing me to hear his actual, unaltered voice. It is slightly higher pitched and has a pleasing timbre. He speaks with an easy cadence that has a smooth, almost hypnotic quality to it. And I was right; he sounds refined and cultured. It could be an affectation, but I get a charge out of knowing that my initial instincts and impressions were correct.

"So what occasions this call, Mr. Hayes?" I ask.

"I wanted to know if you had checked out those names I provided you?"

"I did, actually," I reply. "And those three were just the tip of the iceberg, as it turned out."

He laughs softly on the other end of the line. "So, you've learned my secret."

"I have."

"And what is that secret?" he asks. "Not that I do not believe you of course."

"Trust but verify, right?"

"Something like that," he says. "So? What have you found?"

"That you have been killing for a very long time," I say. "At least twenty-two years, by my count."

There's a soft chuckle on the other end of the line. "A little bit longer than that, actually."

I was right. Those three from 1998 weren't his first kills. The confirmation sends a charge through me that I know I shouldn't be feeling but can't help feeling anyway. Blake would kick me in the balls and probably call me a sociopath for being excited but being on the trail of a serial killer lights me up.

"How many bodies have you discovered, Paxton?" he asks. "May I call you Paxton? I feel as if we are close enough already to be on a first name basis."

"Whatever makes you happy," I reply. "And to answer your question, I've found thirty-six so far."

He chuckles again. "I am impressed."

I shift on my feet and move the phone to my other ear,

keeping an eye on the street around me. Maybe it's my paranoia getting the best of me, but I suddenly get the feeling that I'm being watched. I cut my eyes one way, then the other, but foot traffic is light, and I don't see anybody that stands out, so I allow myself to relax slightly.

"Are there more?" I ask.

"I suppose you will have to figure that out on your own," he says. "I can't do all of your work for you."

"The three you gave me... they weren't your first, were they?"

I already know the answer, but I want confirmation, and I'm also hoping he'll let something slip. It's a longshot. A man this controlled usually won't let things slip. A man like this will only tell me what he wants me to know. But everybody has an off day, right?

"They were not my first," he confirms. "You are right about that."

"So what year did you first kill?"

"I can't give away all my secrets, Paxton. We barely know each other."

I chuckle. "So this is just foreplay."

"Something like that."

"Then let me ask you this," I start, "why me?"

"What do you mean?"

I watch a young couple stroll by, hand in hand, looking at each other like they're over the moon in love and feel a sharp needle of pain lance my heart. Veronica and I used to look at each other like that. I clear my throat and stuff it all down, locking those emotions back inside their box.

"You were invisible for over twenty years. You killed with impunity and could have gone on for another twenty," I say. "So why did you give me the first three vics? Why did you put me on your trail? Nobody was looking for you, so why did you give yourself away? To me, of all people?"

In the background, I hear the sound of a horn. It's loud, long, and low. Almost like a foghorn. As I listen, it hits me. It's a ferry. That tells me he's somewhere near water. But the Sound is a large place; he could be anywhere along the shore. It makes the area to search smaller, but it's still a haystack, and he is just one needle somewhere in the middle of it.

"Why do you think I told you?" he answers my question with a question.

I look up at the clouds again as I hear a rumble of thunder in the distance. It won't be long before the storm breaks.

"It's not for publicity. You could have gone to the media a long time ago," I muse. "I have to think it's because you believe this is a game you're drawing me into. A battle of wits."

"And why would I do that?" he responds. "Why would I risk capture just for a game?"

"Because you don't believe you'll lose. You think you'll outwit and outsmart me," I reply. "But you think it will be fun and will give you a rush of excitement you haven't felt in a long time."

His laughter is low and rueful sounding, and I bristle. It's not because he's laughing, it's because what I just described, the attributes I just ascribed to him can be turned back onto me. His motives for revealing himself to me are the same as my motives for hunting him. The understanding that I am a lot like this man, that we have more in common than I would have ever guessed, let alone acknowledged, leaves me breathless. For a moment, speechless.

"I sense in you a kindred spirit, Paxton," he says.

"I don't kill people."

"You could," he replies.

"Anybody could."

"Cold. Emotionless. Aloof. You do know how many sociopathic tendencies you exhibit, don't you?" he says. "You're far more likely to kill somebody than your average man on the street."

"Sociopaths aren't capable of compassion. Or empathy," I say. "I am."

"Are you?" he replies. "Or do you just fake it to get by?"

I cringe inwardly, hearing the ring of truth in his words. How often have I faked an emotional response I didn't feel because it was expected of me in whatever social situation I happened to be in? Too often. More often than I can count. Not that I'll ever admit that out loud. Or to him.

That feeling of being observed creeps over me again. I cut a glance around the street. I look up at the darkened windows of the buildings around me, wondering if he's behind one of them. I push the thought away though as ridiculous. And impossible. He cannot be in two places at once, and I distinctly heard the ferry in the background, which I cannot hear from where I am.

"None of that means I'm predisposed to murder," I tell him.

"No, but I know that darkness resides in your soul."

"You seem to know me well," I remark.

"Better than you think. I must admit to a certain level of fascination with you."

"That's sweet. Are you going to ask me to go steady next?"

He chuckles. "Perhaps next time," he says. "I just wanted to call to speak to you for a few minutes. I thought it would be nice if we got to know each other a bit better."

"Then let's sit down over coffee. Talk things out. Bond," I offer. "I can definitely feel a bromance building between us."

"Phone calls will suffice for now," he says. "Have to leave a little something to look forward to, don't we?"

"I suppose so."

"I have a splendid feeling about this, Paxton," he says. "I think it will be quite enjoyable playing this game with you. There has never been a soul I've wanted to play with more."

"I feel special."

"As you should. There are very few in this world whose intellect I respect."

"I guess I'm one of the lucky ones, huh?"

"As I said, I feel a kinship with you. A certain fascination. You might even say it's an obsession." As if his words aren't strange enough on their own, he then starts to sing: "You are an obsession. You're my obsession. Who do you want me to be?"

He lets out a high pitched, tittering giggle. It's creepy and makes my skin crawl. At the same, my head is spinning with the surreal turn this conversation has suddenly taken.

"Wow," I say. "That was... something."

He laughs softly. "Well, I never claimed to be good enough to be on Star Search. But I do well enough to get by."

"That is true."

There's a brief pause on the line, and in the background, I hear the ferry horn going off again. He's got to be close to a terminal for it to be so loud and clear.

"Well, this has been a pleasant conversation, Paxton," he says. "And I look forward to more."

"What makes you think I'm going to play your game?"

I can hear the smile in his voice when he speaks. "Because you and I are more alike than you care to admit," he says. "There is nothing that excites you more than the chase. Nothing gets you off like the thrill of the hunt."

It's eerie how well this man seems to know me. Eerier still how similar he and I actually do seem to be. I can't refute his words. They're true.

"And maybe I needed you in my life just as much as you needed me," he says. "We both needed something to fire us up, didn't we? Something to bring us both back to life?"

As much as it galls me to admit, he's not wrong. Again. It galls me to be so similar to a man who's murdered at least thirty-six people. I know I'm not him. That I'm not a killer. But having so much in common with a man who is a killer is disquieting. To say the least. I would be lying if I said it didn't leave me feeling a little bit rattled.

"I will be speaking with you again soon, Paxton," he says. "You have a pleasant evening."

The line goes dead in my hands, and I stare at my phone for a long moment, processing and digesting the whole conversation. It's only then I realize how stupid I was for not recording it and silently chastise myself. He just caught me flat-footed and unprepared.

I won't let that happen again. Next time, I'll be ready for him.

FOURTEEN

Arrington Investigations; Downtown Seattle

"He's arrogant. Almost narcissistic. He's cold and calculating," I rant. "Condescending, though I think he believes he's being complimentary. He has an overabundance of self-confidence and truly thinks he's the most intelligent person to walk the Earth."

"Oh my God," Brody says. "It's you. You're the killer."

He erupts into laughter that fills the conference room. I cut a glance at Blake, who is physically struggling to keep the smile off her face. It's a fight she ultimately loses, and she bursts into laughter as long and loud as Brody's. I roll my eyes at her and wave them off.

"Et tu, Brute?"

"Oh come on, that was funny," she points out. "Lighten up, Arrington. Learn to laugh at yourself a bit."

I lean back in my chair and take a drink of my coffee, letting them have their moment. I'm not amused by the reminder of how similar to this man I am. It's something that kept me up for a good chunk of the night obsessing about it. Finally, their laughter fades, and they sit up, doing their best to keep the smirks off their faces. An endeavor they're not even close to being successful at.

I look at the notes we've written and pictures taped to the whiteboard at the front of the room. We've turned our client conference room into our makeshift HQ. Blake was finally given the green light to look into Hayes — though she was ordered to do it quietly and discreetly — but she's been able to add to our cache of information with the case files she pulled. No doubt, if we make an arrest, they'll trumpet that so loud, they'd probably hear it in China.

It's being classified as an unofficial investigation for the moment, and Blake isn't being given any additional manpower to look into it. But that's fine. More people will only get in our way. The last thing I want is to have to explain— and defend— my participation to a hundred other people. I have a hard enough time keeping Blake off my back about it.

"Okay, so what else can you tell us about him?" Blake asks.

"I'm putting him in his mid-to-late forties—"

"Why is that?" Brody interrupts.

"His references. He sang a line from an eighties song— "Obsession" by a group called Animotion—"

"Wait, he sang you a song?" Brody smirks.

I roll my eyes. "He sang a line from that song. I don't know why."

"This is getting creepier and more bizarre by the minute," he chuckles.

"You don't know how creepy. You didn't have to hear it live," I tell him with a smirk.

"Thank God," he replies.

"What was the line?" Blake asks, her interest piqued.

I recite the line for her. "You are an obsession. You're my obsession. Who do you want me to be?"

"Wow. Sounds like he's got a mancrush on you, Pax," Brody raises an eyebrow. "Sounds like if he has his way, you're going to be picking out china together soon enough."

"I don't think that's how he meant it though," I reply. "In the context of the conversation, it's more a case of he's intrigued by me. Says he's obsessed with my intellect. Somebody he thinks can challenge him. Match wits with him."

"Yeah, that's not arrogant or anything."

"I'd say it sounds we're dealing with a malignant narcissist," Blake adds.

"You're talking about the killer and not Pax, right?" Brody chimes in.

A small and unexpected laugh bursts from my

throat. Even when I'm irritated and trying to focus on something, every once in a while, something Brody says will hit me when I least expect it. Even a joke he might have cracked just minutes before. I don't know; maybe it's a tension reliever. Sort of like turning the pressure release valve in my brain before I hit critical mass. Maybe Brody recognizes that in me, and that's why he's always popping off and trying to keep the mood light around me. Maybe he sees that darkness inside of me that Hayes referred to and does what he can to mitigate it.

"I don't think it's that simple," I say.

"No?"

I shake my head and screw up my face, trying to order my thoughts so I can recount the conversation on the fly, once again kicking myself for not recording the conversation so I could just play certain parts for them.

"He said that he respects my intellect and that I'm the first person in a long time he thought could challenge him," I explain.

"So this is all a game to him," Blake notes. "And you're the only worthy player."

I nod. "Something like that."

"But that fits because this is less about your intellect and how your intellect matches his. The impact you have on him," she continues. "This is all about him and his wants, and really has little to do with you, Pax. You just happened to be the person who clicked with him. This is his game, and you're just a bit player."

I take a moment to digest her words and realize what she's saying makes perfect sense. As I replay the conversation over in my mind, I see that she's right. This really is all about him. I don't know how I didn't see that before.

She smirks. "He really is your Moriarty."

"Yeah, I had that thought too."

"What's a Moriarty?" Brody asks.

I roll my eyes. "Never mind."

He looks at me for a moment with narrowed eyes and pursed lips, then blows out a breath and waves me off, irritated. I chuckle, which earns me another baleful look.

"How do you figure he's in his forties though?" Blake asks.

"The references. The song. It's from 1984. He also mentioned Star Search," I say. "It was some talent show back in the eighties. He seems comfortable in that decade. My guess is that he was a kid back then. Which, if true, would put him in his forties today."

Blake nods. "Not bad, Arrington. Not bad at all."

"Wow man," Brody pipes up. "You do have a brain in that head of yours. I'm impressed."

I shrug. "It narrows certain things down. But age is the hardest thing to predict anyway," I say. "It could be helpful, but we shouldn't necessarily get hung up on it."

"What else did he say?" asks Blake.

I run a hand through my hair as I think. Some of what he said I don't want to repeat. Not until I've had some time to sit with it and think or wrap my head around it all anyway. Some of it I may never want to talk about.

"Oh, I heard the ferry in the background," I tell them. "So he's got to be somewhere close to the Sound. Judging by how loud it was, I'd say he's near a ferry terminal."

"That narrows it down," Brody groans.

"It does, actually," Blake says. "At least we have a specific geographical region as opposed to having to cover the whole state. We know he's local."

"That's true," Brody acknowledges. "Good point."

"For now," I reply. "Given that he's killed all around the West Coast, he may not stay here long. Though I suspect this is his home base. He always returns here."

"What makes you think that?" Brody asks.

"Just a hunch," I reply. "Just a feeling."

"So far, your feelings have been pretty decent," Blake says.

Brody's phone rings. The sudden, shrill bleating in the stillness of the room is jarring, and all three of us jump. He scrambles and is able to silence it quickly. He looks at the display screen, and I see that familiar, goofy smile on his face. Turning his phone face down, he raises his gaze to mine. I just chuckle.

"Go," I say.

"Don't need to tell me twice," he says.

Brody grabs his phone and dashes out of the conference room, stopping by his office, before darting to the elevators. Brody likes to be able to come and go as he pleases, and I don't have a problem with it simply because when there is work I need him to do, I can count on him one hundred percent of the time. I know he's not real thrilled with what we're doing right now. Chasing a serial killer isn't his thing. But if I need any background details, digital records, or anything tech-related, he's there, no questions asked.

"What was that about?" Blake asks.

"He's apparently got a nooner."

She nods. "A little afternoon delight, huh?"

"Skyrockets in flight."

She laughs and shakes her head as I drink my coffee. She looks over as her laughter tapers off, then stops, and I can see her scrutinizing me. I hate the way she does that. She looks into me like she can see right through to my very soul. Can discern my every feeling and my every thought. And it's annoying because she's usually right on the money about whatever it is she's seeing inside of me.

"What aren't you saying?" she asks.

"Why can't you stop reading my mind?"

"What can I say? I'm fascinated by blank pages."

"You're a jerk," I laugh.

"I learn from the best," she replies pointedly. "So come on. What is it? Something he said obviously has you rattled."

I tear strips off the cardboard sleeve on my cup, frowning as I think about it. I haven't gotten a firm hold on the things running through my head yet. I don't particularly want to talk about it until I do. But if there's one person in this world I can talk to, it's Blake. I don't think I can even share what's going through my head with Brody. As much as I love and trust the guy, he's a clown and would rather laugh and joke things off, rather than have a serious talk and figure them out.

But Blake is different. Even if she can't relate to something, she's got a keen mind. She's sharp and sees things differently. Blake is definitely an outside the box thinker, and that's one of the reasons I think she's an excellent FBI agent. Things aren't just black and white to her; she sees all the shades of gray in between.

So I tell her. I recite the whole conversation, start to finish. Having hyperthymesia comes in handy sometimes. And when I'm done, she sits back and stares at me with a thoughtful expression on her face for a long moment, that big brain of hers working overtime.

"You do know you're nothing like him," she starts. "You know that, right?"

A wry smile touches my lips. "Honestly, I am," I reply. "He pretty much described me to a T."

"Except for the fact that you're not a killer."

"He thinks I can be."

She arches her eyebrow. "You think he's trying to groom you?"

I shrug. "Maybe."

"Or maybe he's just trying to get into your head, Pax."

"That could be too. I guess it worked," I admit. "But he's honestly not wrong. There are a lot of similarities between us."

"But you have the ability to show compassion and empathy," she presses. "True sociopaths don't."

"I fake it, Blake. I don't feel those things," I sigh. "I just learned to mimic those emotions well enough to get by."

She sits back in her chair and takes in what I just said, looking a bit stunned and a little shocked by it. I know the feeling.

"I could be just like him with one push the wrong way," I tell her.

She shakes her head. "That's bull. You have got one of the strongest moral compasses of anybody I've ever known."

"Do I though? Do I really?" I ask. "I lie. I manipulate people to get my way. Like you tell me over and over, I'm arrogant."

She cocks her head and looks at me. "And none of that makes you a killer. The defining trait is that you know right from wrong, and you may dance on that line, but you never cross it," she urges. "Jesus, this guy did a number on you. I've never seen you doubt yourself like this."

I don't know that I've ever doubted myself like this before. And yeah, Hayes did do a number on me. She's right about that. He nudged me toward thoughts I've had all my life but have tried to stifle and ignore. But there are times, usually when I'm alone and my mood is dark, that I wonder if I could do the unthinkable. There have been times in my life when I've wondered if I could actually do it. If I could take a human life. Times I've wondered if I could kill and keep killing.

I never talk about it. I don't share that side of myself with anybody. I never even told Veronica I'd had those thoughts when I was younger. I figured it would scare her. That I would scare her. When we got together though, those thoughts all went away. It was like magic. My mind was finally quiet, I felt at peace, and I never thought about whether or not I had what it took to be a serial killer again.

Not until Hayes brought it up last night. It was like pulling the scab off an old wound. And now my mind is festering with those thoughts, and that terrible darkness is once more covering me like a shroud.

"I can prove to you in one single word that Hayes is wrong, and you're not a sociopath," Blake says.

"One word, huh?"

"Veronica."

"And that proves... what exactly?"

A small smile pulls the corners of her mouth upward. "It proves that you have the capacity for genuine human emotion. That you have the capacity for love," she says. "Unless, of course, you were faking it with her?"

Growing up as an Arrington meant that my life was filled with forced social interactions. I was expected to speak and behave in a certain way. I was forced to observe certain social norms and know my social graces, even if I despised the person I was being forced to interact with. Being an Arrington meant I had to fake my way through most of my life.

But that all changed with Veronica. She saw through the facade and never demanded that I be anything but who I am— who I really am— with her. She would not tolerate that genteel veneer that being an Arrington requires. She was the first person who wanted me to be me. Just Pax. Not Paxton Arrington, heir to a media empire. And I loved her for that. I never had to put on airs or pretenses with her. For the first time in my life, I could just be me and that was enough. I was enough.

A wan smile crosses my face. "No, I wasn't faking it with her," I say quietly. "I loved her with everything in me. I still do."

"And that right there proves that you are nothing like Hayes."

"Yeah, maybe."

"I won't deny that you check a lot of boxes on the sociopath profile. I've said that for a while," she says.

"Pretty much from the day we met."

She laughs softly. "Okay, that's fair," she replies. "But what I'm saying is that the similarities between you and Hayes are what will allow us to catch him."

"What makes you say that?"

"Because you know how he thinks," she says. "You'll be able to predict his actions."

"I think I'll be able to better predict his actions based on his behavior more than our shared personality flaws."

"So you're a profiler now, are you?"

I flash her a grin. "Couldn't be any worse at it than you feebs," I crack. "After all, I am smarter than you lot."

"There's the cocky bastard I know and adore."

Talking it out with Blake has helped settle my mind. At least, somewhat. But I'm feeling a bit better about things, and not like I'm teetering on the edge of becoming a serial killer anytime soon. She's given me some much-needed perspective. Which is one of the things I appreciate most about Blake: her level-headedness. That and her willingness to give me a swift kick in the butt when I need it.

"Thank you, Blake," I smile.

"Anytime, Pax."

FIFTEEN

REUBEN HAYES

Bainbridge Island, WA

I sit on the back deck of my home, enjoying a glass of *Chateau Pontet-Canet* Cabernet and another dazzling sunset. The storm passed, leaving the sky streaked with thin, wispy clouds that glow in vibrant shades of orange and red. The sun sparkles off the surface of the Sound, making it glitter like a pool of liquid fire. I take a sip and breathe in the ocean air, savoring it every bit as much as this glass of wine.

I spent a good part of the day watching the footage from Paxton's office. I was curious to know what they had to say in the wake of my conversation with him last night. And I wasn't disappointed. They had a lot of interesting things to say, and I enjoyed their breakdown and analysis of our little chat.

What I didn't appreciate, though, was the woman

talking him down. I want— no, I need— for Paxton to be on edge. I need him to let his inner darkness out to play. I want him to eventually understand what it is I am doing. And why I'm doing it. If there's anybody who can grasp the scope of my work and appreciate it, it will be Paxton Arrington.

He is a mirror image of me. Whether he accepts it or not, he and I are more alike than we're not. The more I've learned about Paxton, the more I've come to see that like me, he's got a strong moral compass. He has a certainty about what's right and what's wrong. And he has an intellect far superior to most people. Just like me. And all he needs is a gentle nudge in the right direction, a little guidance, and he'll see that what I'm doing is right. He'll pick up my mantle.

I did not know it at first. I did not see it. I was taken by his intellect, and of course, the coincidence of sharing a passion for the Sherlock Holmes books made it seem more like serendipity. I thought I finally had somebody to challenge me. Revealing my kills and putting him on my trail is risky. It was impulsive; something I rarely ever am. I am always in such tight control of myself. I do not take risks. That is why I've been able to conduct my work for more than twenty years.

But over time, I must admit that my work has lost much of its flavor. The work is necessary, and I still take pride in what I do, but it's become too easy. Too perfunctory. Maybe I've lost a bit of my edge, but I haven't gotten any true enjoyment out of it in years. In

Paxton, though, I thought I found somebody who would push me intellectually. Somebody who might challenge me and renew that thrill. That rush of adrenaline I used to get when I was doing my work. And that set me on fire inside in ways I haven't felt since... well, since that October night all those years ago. It is a high I have been chasing since that night, in fact.

But the more I learn about Paxton, the more I think he's meant to do more than just push and challenge me, although that is part of his role in my life. He's exceptional. He reminds me of my younger self in so many ways. And it's for that reason I believe he's meant to become me. He's meant to undergo a metamorphosis and emerge with his eyes open, his heart clear, and his mission firmly in mind. Like I did all those years ago. I can feel it.

The final test, of course, will be the game. I have to make certain he's worthy of becoming me. Worthy of inheriting my mantle and continuing my work. I must ensure that he is worthy of building upon my legacy. If he survives, he's worthy. If he dies, he wasn't.

But that woman, FBI Special Agent Blake Wilder, is a wild card and she is standing in my way. Standing in Paxton's way of becoming what he is meant to be. She's going to be a problem I need to do something about. But what? What can I do about her? How should I handle her without bringing the FBI's resources to bear on me?

She's not a woman I can frighten or intimidate. And yet, she is not a woman I wish to kill, either. She seems to be a morally righteous woman, and though I doubt she isn't without some skeletons in her closet, they likely wouldn't rise to the level I require for judgment. Even I have standards and morals. But I might not have a choice if she proves to be too much of a problem for me. There are events in motion that are too important to stop now. Too important to let anybody get in the way of.

That's when it hits me. A way to solve all of my problems at once. The thought of it brings a smile to my face as the idea starts to take shape in my mind. I still need to flesh out the finer points, of course, but I think this is workable. I think this is very workable.

And it will tell me whether or not Paxton is actually worthy to carry on my mission.

SIXTEEN
PAXTON

Archton Media Archives Room, Downtown Seattle

"Afternoon, Mr. Arrington," he says. "Long time, no see."

"How are you today, Archie?"

"Can't complain," he grins. "Much."

I give him a smile. Archie has been working security at the Archton Building for twenty-five years. He's a huge, burly man who, once upon a time, was one of the best defensive linemen in all of college football. A busted-up knee kept him from making the jump to the pros, but he never let himself get bitter about it. As long as I've known him— which is most of my life— he's always been amicable and always has a smile on his face.

"How's Connie doing?"

"Still ruling with an iron fist."

"As she should," I reply. "Somebody has to keep you in line."

"Your mouth to God's ear."

We share a laugh. His wife Connie is definitely the tough, strong one in their relationship and never lets him get away with anything. She's a great lady, but one I would not want to be on the wrong side of.

"So what can I help you with today?" he asks.

"Just need to get into the morgue."

"You got it."

Archie hands me the access key for the elevator needed to get to the subterranean floors where they keep scads of information that never made it to print or on-air, in a room filled with air-gapped computers. My father reasons that since digital data is easy to store, there's no reason to dump it, since you never know when it might be relevant to another story again. I'm suddenly glad he's a digital hoarder like that.

"Thanks, Archie."

"Anytime, Mr. Arrington."

I take the elevator down to sub-level three and step out, passing through rows and rows of servers, all of them humming. I use my keycard to unlock the door to the Vault, where the computers are stored. The room is a plexiglass box, and with the fluorescent lights overhead and a pristine tile floor that gleams startlingly white. I have to cover my eyes for a moment. I pick a computer station, take off my jacket and hang it on the back of the chair, then sit down and get to work.

I call up the in-house search program and start inputting data, keywords, and anything else I can think of. I know that I'm basically looking for another needle in another haystack, but I can't sit around waiting and hoping the answers will fall into my lap. I need to be doing something.

I start combing through all of the information I can find on the six original murders. The ones that continue to haunt Blake. I call up everything I can find on them, reading every article, watching every clip, and sifting through everything that was never used. I don't know exactly what it is I'm searching for, but I'm hoping something clicks. Regardless, having as much background information as possible can't be a bad thing. The more I know, the better.

"Heard you were in the building."

I look up, surprised I hadn't heard the door to the Vault open, then cut a quick glance at my watch, surprised to see that four hours have elapsed since I walked in. I guess I've been so consumed in what I'm doing, I've shut everything else out. I've consumed a ton of information, but I don't know that any of it will be particularly relevant. Which is disappointing but not wholly unexpected.

"Hey Dad," I say. "How are you?"

"I'm fine, son," he replies. "Just wondering what you're doing down here."

"Research."

"For what?"

"A case I'm working."

He nods. "Right. You're still doing that private investigator thing."

I chuckle softly. "I am."

My father is a tall, thin man. If I were to describe him in one word, I suppose it would have to be 'stately'. His hair is silver, his features chiseled, and his eyes are a slightly darker shade of green than mine. His frame is slight, and he's not intimidating at all, but he has a presence and a gravitas about him that can't be denied. He dominates any room he walks into. If Central Casting came calling for somebody to play the president, I have no doubt my father would land the role.

He sighs and sits down on the corner of the desk I'm working at, staring down at me, his eyes boring into mine. I know what he wants to say. Know what he wants me to do. I'm not like my brother, though, who my father can seemingly force to do anything with nothing but that steely-eyed gaze.

"Are you going to make me ask?" he finally says.

"No, there's no reason for you to ask, Dad," I say. "I'm not going to do it. I have no interest in running Archton. Zero. Zip. None."

"Be reasonable, Paxton," he replies. "This is where you belong. You've proven yourself—"

"So has George. He's done everything you've ever asked him to do," I tell him. "He's smart. Driven. Ambitious. He has a lot of great ideas for the future of the company if you'd actually listen to him for a change."

"I love your brother; you know that—"

"It has nothing to do with whether you love him or not. I know you do," I say. "It has to do with him being the better man to run Archton than me. He has the desire and the ability to do it, Dad. I don't."

He looks at me for a long moment, his eyes filled with sadness. I swear, the way he's looking at me makes me feel like somebody just died. And who knows, maybe he feels that way. I know he's wanted me to follow in his footsteps. He's been pressuring me since I was a kid to get a good education, get good grades, to prove myself capable of leading the company into the future.

And for so long, I tried to fit that mold. I went to the best schools and got good grades. I did everything I needed to do to prove myself to my father, just like I was supposed to do. But then I met Veronica and everything changed. She opened my eyes to things and got me thinking about things in ways I never had before. Much to my father's chagrin.

The disappointment is etched into his face. But really, he couldn't have expected anything different. I've been putting him off for ten years now, telling him I have no interest in sliding into his spot when he steps down. He's refused to hear me. But maybe now that he's getting near the age where he's thinking about his own future and how he wants to spend his golden years, it's finally starting to sink in. I think for the first time, he's finally understanding that I want to walk my own path and chart my own course through life.

My father stands and slips his hands into his pockets. I can still see the disappointment in his eyes, but his expression takes on a different look. It's one I know well. It's what I like to call his, 'frustrated and angry, about to make some incomprehensible and long-winded point about nothing', face. I've been seeing it since I was a kid. He makes that face every time he thinks he can bully and badger me into something.

"You know, you started to change when you met that girl—"

"Dad, don't start. Don't even go there," I snap. "Don't you dare bring her into this. You have no right."

I grit my teeth and try to tamp down the anger that's flaring inside of me. I'm outraged that he would dare invoke Veronica's memory. I take a moment to focus on my breath and force myself to stay calm. Blowing up at him isn't going to do anything but inflame this situation, and that's the last thing I want.

He and my mother never approved of me marrying Veronica. Oh, they said all the right things, of course. The Arringtons are nothing if not socially graceful at all times. They were always nice enough to Veronica, but they never really made her feel like she was a part of the family. Not really. They never thought she was good enough for me. That I was marrying down. That I could do better and that I should be marrying somebody of means, of a proper social station.

When she died, they almost seemed relieved. Again, they said and did all the right things, made all of the socially required gestures. But it wasn't as if they were hurting. Not like I was. They weren't hurting as if they had lost a family member. To me, they were acting as if Veronica was just a girl I'd broken up with. Not a wife who had died.

"All I'm saying is that when you met her, you changed, son," he says. "You started to distance yourself from your family. You turned your back on us, Pax."

"I didn't turn my back on you, Dad," I tell him. "I just found another path."

"Your path should have led you here."

"You're the one who always told me how critical it is that I be my own man and think for myself," I snap. "And now you're giving me crap because I did what you always taught me to do?"

He sighs. I can see him physically trying to restrain himself. To control his frustration and his anger with me.

"The family is still important to me, Dad. It always will be. My family is everything to me," I continue. "But I have a different way of seeing things. A different way of doing things. And rather than punish me for it, you should welcome it. You should be happy to know you raised a strong, independent man who is nobody's puppet. I think for myself."

He looks away from me and closes his mouth, biting back the scathing reply I know was sitting on the tip of his tongue. He finally looks at me for a long moment, his lips pursed, not saying a word. The silence is suffocating and oppressive. Part of me wants to say something simply to ease the quiet tension.

But I recognize this as just another one of my father's tactics. It's almost a battle of wills with him. He makes the tension so unbearable and uncomfortable that it puts you on your heels and gives him the upper hand. And then, when he has you reeling, he will badger and bully you. Eventually, you're so frazzled that you agree just to make him stop. I've seen him do it countless times.

I'm not going to give into him though. Not this time. I know who I am and know where I stand on things. Where I stand on my life. This push and pull between us has been going on for a long time now, but this time there seems to be a sense of finality in it. An understanding and perhaps a grudging acceptance.

Perhaps seeing that he isn't going to break my resolve, my father gets to his feet and walks out of the Vault without another word, leaving me alone in the silent room.

"Well, the next family dinner should be fun," I muse to myself.

SEVENTEEN

Outside the Emerald Rainbow Motel, Seattle, WA

"The guy is worth millions and he can't spring for a decent hotel?" I mutter.

I'm sitting in my Navigator in a darkened parking lot across the street from the Emerald Rainbow Motel. The apparent love nest of Murray Taub, founder and CEO of the Queen City Steakhouse, and his eighteen-year-old, fresh out of high school sweetheart, who after doing some digging, I've learned is Tandy Sellers.

He's a portly man who looks like he's one or two more of his steaks away from a stroke. Tandy looks like the head cheerleader/prom queen type. She's a tall, lean, blonde, blue-eyed, beauty. She's a beautiful girl, and I can't see her relationship with ol' Murray as anything but an attempt at a cash grab.

He's probably giving her the 'I'm going to leave my

wife and marry you', line and she's probably buying it, envisioning a life on Easy Street. She might be willing to trade an hour of his sweaty, porcine body on top of hers a few times a week in exchange for a maid, an Amex Black Card, and a closet full of shoes and clothes.

And if that's the case, more power to her. I'm not going to judge the girl for that. I just think it's incredibly naive and shows a complete lack of awareness of how the world works. It's a shame she's going to learn a really hard lesson like this, but it's apparently a lesson she's got to learn. If the guy won't even take her to a decent hotel, it shows what he thinks of her. At least, that's what I think.

With everything going on, I'd put Mrs. Taub and her pending divorce filing on the back burner. I was reminded when she called me this morning to read me the riot act for not having the evidence she needs for her case. Luckily for me, Mr. Taub is still in the honeymoon phase with his prom queen and still seeing her most nights.

I've already gotten some pretty incriminating shots of the happy couple, but I need a few more just to put the icing on the cake and make sure Mrs. Taub is happy with her divorce settlement. But they just went into the room a few minutes ago, so it's going to be a while yet.

I sit back in my seat and turn on the interior light, pulling open the satchel on the seat next to me, and slip the file out. I look down at the tattered and worn edges and knowing what's inside, feel a punch to the gut every bit as hard today as I did that day two years ago. The pain and the hurt haven't diminished one iota. Some days, I wonder if it ever will. Some days I think whoever said time heals all wounds was a liar.

Despite being able to recite the contents of every report, summary, and scrap of paper inside the file backwards and forwards, I scan through it again. I look at the photos, trying to see them from a different angle. Trying to find the one thing I know I must have missed inside those pages that will blow the lid off everything.

I don't believe the official report of Veronica's death. Most everybody I know has said it's a natural mark of grief. That I'm still stuck in the denial stage. I'm not saying I won't accept the official conclusion at some point. But that point won't come until I've exhausted every avenue, reconciled every discrepancy, and accounted for every last thing that doesn't sit right with me. Once I can't find a single loose thread in the official theory of Veronica's death, I'll accept their conclusions. But not a minute before then.

I tried to get SPD to look at it closer while I was still with the department. I rattled every cage I could think of to get somebody to look at Veronica's case. To a man, they all said there was no case to be had. They wrote it off as a simple accident caused by an unfortunate patch of black ice on a cold winter night.

It didn't matter that although, yes, it was cold that night, it was not black ice cold. The temperature was above freezing. Thirty-four degrees, by all weather reports of that evening. And yet despite that fact, I'm supposed to believe she hit a patch of black ice, lost control of her car, and ended up going end over end, the crushed and twisted metal of her car ending up in a ditch.

I had an independent inspector look over the car to see if he could determine what had happened and what caused the accident. Unfortunately, the damage was too extensive for him to make any sort of concrete determination. Nor did he want to speculate about the cause of the crash from a mechanical standpoint.

I was left frustrated and without any answers as to why my beautiful wife, the woman who showed me a better way to live, the woman who saved me, died. It was the one time I thought about leveraging my family name to compel somebody to look into Veronica's case. Ultimately, I didn't do it. I couldn't justify using my family's name and stature within the city to force the SPD to do my bidding. It was tempting, but I couldn't do it.

So I've spent the last two years searching for answers on my own, and have come up dry at every turn. And as I study the last photo carefully, searching for the smallest detail I might have missed in the last ten million times I've scrutinized it; I blow out a frustrated breath. I close the file and slip it back into my satchel just as I see the door to Taub's hotel room open. I glance at my watch and see that it's only been thirty minutes.

"Disappointing performance, Mr. Taub," I say.

"You're going to have to do better than that to keep an eighteen-year-old girl's interest."

I pick up my camera and take aim, making sure I zoom in on the couple as they lean against the car, kissing each other passionately. I make sure I get a close up of their faces, so there is no doubt. As Murray pulls back, a lecherous smile on his face, I see a flash of disgust cross Tandy's face. It's brief and is quickly replaced by a wide, bright smile, but it confirms for me that my original thinking about her stake in this relationship was correct.

I chuckle to myself as I put my camera down. I do so enjoy being correct. I'm just about to pack it in for the night when my cellphone rings. I pick it up and see the call is coming from a restricted number and immediately feel a jolt. I have no reason to think it, but I just have a feeling I know who's on the other end of the line, so I connect the call.

"Arrington," I answer.

"Paxton, it is good to hear your voice again."

I was right. It's Hayes. A rush of adrenaline flows through me, and I feel that familiar tingle of excitement crawling along my skin.

"Mr. Hayes," I say. "What a surprise."

"I didn't interrupt anything important, did I?"

"No, just documenting the depraved infidelity of an old man."

He chuckles. "I admire your morals, Paxton," he

says. "I appreciate that you have such a strong sense of right and wrong."

"I don't know about all that," I reply. "I was just hired to do a job."

"Don't be modest, Paxton," he insists. "You have a very strong moral compass."

"Yeah, I guess," I say. "Tell me something, is that why you do what you do? Because of your strong moral compass?"

"Of course."

"I can't help but notice the religious overtones—"

He laughs softly, cutting me off.

"Is something funny?" I ask.

"Religion can be a violent and destructive thing," he says. I can't help but hear the note of bitterness in his voice. "It can be vile and oppressive."

"So why the religious iconography at your murder scenes?" I ask. "Why the crosses?"

"Call it my own personal peccadillo," he replies.

In the motel parking lot, Taub has Tandy pressed up against the car and is all over her. She's trying to look like she's enjoying it, but her expression is caught somewhere between revulsion and fear. Poor girl.

"This man whose depraved infidelity you're documenting… does he make you angry?" Hayes asks.

"Not particularly," I reply. "Just kind of repulsed, honestly."

"Curious."

"Why is it curious?"

"I presumed for sure blatant infidelity would upset you."

I chuckle softly. "Not to the point that I'd, say, kill him," I say. "If that's what you're getting at."

"As you like to say, you can't blame me for trying."

Taub finally disentangles himself from Tandy and steps back. He watches the girl get into her car and shut the door after her before he turns and gets into his Maserati. A midlife crisis car if I've ever seen one.

"What can I do for you tonight, Mr. Hayes?"

"I was just doing some reading, actually," he says. "About your wife. A fascinating story. I didn't actually think it would be relevant, but I was wrong."

The adrenaline that flows through me is electric. My stomach churns, and my heart stutters. I want to hear Veronica's name passing his lips even less than I wanted to hear it coming out of my father's.

"What about her?" I ask.

"I just thought it was such a tragic loss to have to endure," he says. "I am truly sorry for that."

"Yeah, I don't want to talk about that."

"From what I've gathered, she had a profound impact on you," he continues. "Changed the course of your life."

"You speak as if you know me."

"Well, in some ways I do," he says. "Perhaps even better than you know yourself."

"Yeah, whatever you say," I reply. "But like I said, I don't want to talk about it."

"She must have been a very special—"

"Drop it, Hayes. Now."

He falls silent, but I can sense his amusement on the other end of the line. He's enjoying this. I redirect my attention and watch as Taub pulls out of the parking lot and drives down the street, moving quickly, leaving me alone with the sociopath on the phone. Thanks, Murray. I grit my teeth, doing my best to not let him get to me. He's trying to get into my head, and I can't give him the satisfaction. I won't.

"Do you think you knew her well?" he presses. "Veronica, that is. Do you think you knew everything there was to know about her?"

"I don't think we ever truly know everything about another person," I reply. "Not even somebody we're married to. Nor should we. We all need our secrets and those things that are ours and ours alone."

"I suppose that's true," he replies. "But do you think you knew her well?"

"Of course I did," I snap. "She was my wife."

"Interesting. You're very defensive of her. Even still. I rather like that. It shows loyalty," he notes. "I will be interested to see if that is actually true."

I take a breath and let it out slowly, recognizing that he's trying to get under my skin. A sardonic grin pulls the corners of my mouth upward as I realize how similar to my father he is in that regard, both always poking and prodding around the edges, trying to get under my skin in an effort to bend me to their will.

"Was there a reason for this call?" I ask. "Or do you just enjoy the sound of my voice?"

"You know, I have been trying to figure how exactly Special Agent Wilder fits into our burgeoning narrative," he says.

The mention of Blake's name rattles me. I have to keep myself from responding or giving any indication that he'd caught me off guard. I don't know how it is he knows about Blake and me. It's not as if we spend a lot of time out in public together. So even if he was tailing me, the odds of him seeing us together are slim. Either my luck is really that bad, or the answer is something much simpler and disturbingly devious.

"Oh, we have a burgeoning narrative, do we?" I ask, hoping my voice doesn't give me away.

If what I'm thinking is true, I don't want to tip my hand just yet. I don't want Hayes to know that I'm onto him. Or give him any ideas if I'm not.

"Surely you feel it building," he says with a chuckle. "And in our narrative, I had originally thought Special Agent Wilder was your Watson."

"I assume you have since rethought that opinion, and you're just dying to share it with me; otherwise, you wouldn't have brought it up."

"Indeed," he says. "I have become convinced that she is your Irene Adler."

"Is that so?"

"Does that not please you?"

"This is real life," I tell him. "Not fiction."

"This is the great game."

I lean my head back against the headrest and close my eyes. "I've told you before that I'm not playing your game," I tell him. "I am going to find you, though. I am going to put an end to you and bring your mission to an end."

"I am trying to teach you something, Paxton. I am trying to show you just how powerful you can become," he says. "I'm trying to teach you that you can be so much more than you are."

"Believe it or not, I'm just fine as I am."

He laughs softly. "Your eyes just need to be opened," he says. "You need to be shown that you are worthy."

Being worthy in this man's eyes is the last thing I want or need. I hate that I feel the darkness inside of roiling and churning like cold, greasy snakes in the pit of my belly because of him. I hate feeling drawn to him. And I really hate, more than anything, that all of those feelings that were once such a part of me, feelings Veronica once helped banish, have been reawakened because of this man.

"I've already told you that I am not going to play your game," I growl.

"Oh, but you already are," he coos. "Even if you don't realize it yet."

EIGHTEEN

The Pulpit; Downtown Seattle

"Irene Adler?"

I nod and settle back into the booth as I sip on my glass of scotch. Distaste twists Blake's features.

"He's really taking this whole Sherlock aesthetic a bit too far, don't you think?" she asks.

"It's apparently important to him for some reason," I shrug.

"It's because it's what bonded you two together in the first place," she points out. "He's holding tightly to that."

"A little too tightly, if you ask me," I say. "As much as I was obsessed with the books as a kid, I don't need to center my life around it."

She shakes her head. "That's not it. He's not

centering his life around it. Just his relationship with you."

"Which somehow seems creepier."

Blake gives me a smile. "It only needs to make sense to him."

"Yeah, I guess so."

Blake takes a drink of her club soda— no alcohol for her while she's on duty— and screws up her face in concentration.

"Wasn't Irene Adler Holmes' girlfriend?" she asks. "I mean, Hayes knows we're not together like that, right?"

I shake my head. "In the books themselves, they weren't together. She was his foil, and they had a deep, mutual respect for one another," I tell her. "It's only in the bastardized Hollywood versions of the books that they've injected sexual tension between them."

"Thanks for that history lesson I didn't need or want."

I laugh softly. "Hey, you asked."

I see Brody come through the front doors of the bar and beeline straight over to us. He slides into the booth next to Blake, an expression of excitement on his face. He's practically bouncing up and down like a kid on Christmas morning.

"So?" I ask.

"Swept the whole office," he says. "You were right."

"Of course I was," I say. "Did you doubt me?"

Blake looks between us, an expression of confusion on her face. "You boys going to tell me what's going on?"

I look over at her and grin. "Did it not occur to you to wonder how he knew who you were?" I ask. "How he knew your name? I certainly never mentioned you to him."

Blake sits back in her seat, a dumbfounded expression crossing her face for a moment as the implications of it all sink in for her.

"You're kidding me," she says. "He bugged your office?"

Brody produces a clear plastic bag and shakes it before dropping it onto the table between us with a metallic thud. I pick up the bag and study the contents, shaking my head, then cast a look at Brody.

"Nah, we're good. I made sure they're all junk now," Brody says. "But how did he get these into the office?"

"I should have known."

"Should have known what?" Blake asks.

"The computer repairman," I say. "The same guy was at the Morgans' house doing cable repair. He was wearing a disguise, but I should have seen through it."

"How could you have?" Blake asks. "There's no way you could have known we'd be here right now."

"Yeah, but—"

"She's right, man," Brody says. "There's no way you could have known any of this would happen."

"So he's been listening to us this whole time. He knows everything we do," Blake says.

I nod. "Yeah. Apparently so," I say. "But at least we figured it out before any real damage was done."

"So like, not to be the selfish, self-centered coward here—"

"It's never stopped you before," Blake grins as she cuts Brody off.

"I see those Bureau comedy lessons seem to be paying off," he fires back. "Anyway, now that we've found his stuff, does that make it more likely that he'll be coming after us?"

"Probably not. It just means we need to be very careful about what we say in the office," I reply. "It also means we're going to need to sweep the office every single day, just to be sure he didn't slip in and plant more."

Brody nods, but he looks uneasy about the whole thing. His sense of adventure doesn't usually extend beyond picking up strange women in bars. Blake is looking at the bugs from the office; her face a mixture of consternation and dismay. She drops the bag and raises her gaze to me, her eyes narrow and her jaw set in a line of grim determination.

"What else did you and your new BFF talk about?" Blake asks.

I replay the entire conversation with them, start to finish. They hang on every word. And when I finish, they both look at each other, then turn back to me, both of them looking astounded. And disturbed.

"There's a lot there to unpack, man," Brody whistles low. "I'm going to need some alcohol for this."

He slips out of the booth and heads to the bar, where he immediately strikes up a conversation with a tall, willowy redhead. I roll my eyes and turn back to Blake.

"I guess he'll be otherwise occupied for a while," I say.

"Fine, we'll go on without him."

"So, this isn't a religious thing, huh?"

I shake my head. "His disdain for religion is palpable," I tell her. "You could hear it in his voice."

"So why the crosses?"

"Irony? To make a point?"

My voice tapers off as my head starts to play out all the possibilities. And as I scroll through them all, I come to one inescapable conclusion that I can't ignore.

"He grew up with religion," I state. "Maybe his father was a pastor or something, but he was definitely raised in a religious home."

"What makes you say that?" Blake asks.

"Because only somebody raised in a religious household can have that much contempt for it," I say. "To call it vicious and destructive, vile and oppressive... that can only come from somebody raised in religion. Somebody who was steeped in it every single day and didn't have a very good experience with it."

Blake takes a drink and leans back, seeming to be contemplating my words. She sets her glass down on the table, taking a moment to carefully line it up with the ring of moisture it had left before. Finally, she looks back up at me and nods.

"Yeah, I can see that," she says. "That makes sense. So we need to be searching for bitter, homicidal pastor's sons who are living near a ferry terminal."

"Narrows things down a bit," I say with a laugh.

"Yeah, let me Google that."

We both fall silent for a moment and take a drink, and I let that profile solidify in my head. It seems right to me. It's not complete yet, but it's a good working picture of the man. But I need more. There has to be something more. That one critical piece of information that will lead me to him. As I sit there pondering, I realize how much this situation parallels my situation with Veronica. I'm searching for that one thing, that one piece of information that will open the entire thing up for me.

"So why was he so interested in Veronica?" she asks.

I shake my head. "Just trying to get under my skin," I say. "Like my father sometimes does."

"You have got some complicated, really messed up relationships in your life," she notes. "You know that, don't you?"

"Tell me about it."

"You know what you need?"

"Fewer complications?"

She grins. "Friends. Like, actual friends," she says.

"You need to learn to be social and see what healthy relationships look like."

"You're my friend. So is Brody," I say.

"I'm not around much, and Brody's a clown," she replies. "I'm talking about people who aren't us, who can socialize you. You're like a feral dog right now."

I wave her off. "People are overrated."

"That's why you don't have friends."

"No, I don't have friends because people are petty, ridiculous creatures, and most of them don't have the intellectual capacity to hold my interest for more than five minutes at a time."

"I suppose I should feel special then, considering the length of our friendship," she replies with a smile.

"Yeah, you probably should."

While it's true that I don't need people in general, I do need Brody and Blake. They are, as all the cool kids say, my fam. Aside from Veronica, they're the only two who've ever genuinely gotten me. They understand and accept me as I am; faults, flaws, warts, and all. And really, that's all I need. They're all I need.

"So, what are we going to do about Hayes?"

I shake my head. "I don't know yet. The ball's unfortunately in his court."

"I hate waiting for him to make a move," she says. "I don't like being on the defensive."

"Same. I'd rather be playing offense. But we don't know what we're doing or who we're looking for yet," I sigh. "The answer is going to be found in his early kills. Not the three names he gave me, but before that."

She nods. "If we can figure out who his original victim was, we may be able to put some more pieces into the puzzle and figure out who he is."

"Exactly."

"So how do we do that?" she says with a loud sigh. "He most likely didn't tag his first kill with the flaming cross."

"Probably not," I nod. "So putting them in order by year won't solve our dilemma. I guess I have to hope he calls me again. And that he lets something slip."

"Great," Blake groans. "What a promising plan."

She's not wrong, but until he slips up or we find another clue, we're dead in the water. This is his show, and unfortunately, we've got no choice but to dance to his tune.

NINETEEN

Downtown Seattle

"What's he doin' here?"

"Good to see you too, Matty," I say. "Looks like the nose healed up fine."

"That's Detective Sergeant Schreiber to you," he spits. "And my nose healed up a lot better than your career."

I flash him a grin. "It was so worth it."

"Screw you, Arrington. Get off my crime scene."

"If you boys can't play nice, I'm going to have to put you both in time out."

"He started it," I crack with a smirk on my face.

"Stow it, Arrington," Blake replies, though I hear the laughter in her voice.

I grin as she steps over to us. She looks up at Schreiber, who towers over her by six inches, and yet somehow, it's Blake who seems to be the larger of the two. She's just got that presence about her.

The crime scene is buzzing with activity as uniformed cops bustle about, a couple of them jostling us as they tape off the area and hold back all of the rubberneckers. It makes me think about my own time working in that line. By far the least enjoyable part of the job. There are several blue and whites parked at the scene, as well as a couple of unmarked cars, all of their bubble lights spinning, adding to the chaotic energy of the scene.

Blake called me before the sun was even up this morning to tell me patrol cops had found a dead hooker in an alley who'd been cut up pretty bad. I didn't know she'd set up a Google alert system within the SPD, but it shouldn't surprise me. She can sweet talk people, and with a little well-practiced flirting, I have no doubt she can get the cops to tip her off about almost anything. It's just another one of those things she's got in her toolbox that she uses so well. She's definitely got a finesse and grace about her I'll never have.

"Who are you?" Schreiber growls.

In one smooth, obviously well practiced motion, Blake flips open her creds for him to see. I see Schreiber's eyes tighten and his mouth pucker as his face darkens. It's always a territorial pissing match when the Feds show up. No self-respecting cop likes to have the Feds bigfoot their way onto a case. In this case though, I'm glad she is. If for no other reason than to screw with Schreiber.

"This ain't a federal case," Schreiber says. "It's local. We don't need you—"

"Relax, Detective Sergeant Schreiber. I'm not here to take your case away from you," she cuts in, her tone placating. "This is academic on my behalf."

"This is a crime scene, not a classroom," Schreiber declares. "You can walk yourself back to Quantico if you want to learn something."

A malicious smirk crosses Blake's face as she looks at the angry, red-faced detective. I just stand back, grinning as I watch the show. Schreiber really doesn't know the pile he just stepped in.

"That's Special Agent Wilder, to you," Blake says, her tone harder than steel. "And if you would rather get into a jurisdictional pissing match rather than being reasonable and giving me ten minutes, we can do that. I guarantee though, if I bring the force of the FBI to bear, it's not going to go your way. You will not like how that one ends."

I open my mouth to add my own two cents but close it again when Blake shoots me a withering glare. I slip my hands into my coat pockets and remain silent, looking up at the sky filled with patchy clouds overhead just to make sure I swallow down my remark. When I finally turn back, I see Schreiber's practically turned purple, his face twisted in anger. He's absolutely apoplectic, weighing his options and coming to the realization that he has none. The Feds will win every single time, and he knows it. I enjoy seeing this harsh, brutal side of Blake.

"Fine. You've got ten minutes," he snaps, then points at me. "But he needs to get out of here. He ain't welcome on my crime scene."

"He's consulting for the Bureau," she replies dismissively. "He stays."

Schreiber mutters darkly under his breath and waves us off as he turns and storms away. Blake cuts a glance at me, a grin on her face.

"He's charming," she says. "I don't know why on earth you would have punched a nice guy like that in the face. You really are a monster."

I laugh as I pull out a pair of black nitrile gloves and pull them on. As Blake is gloving up, I look around the alley, feeling a sense of déjà vu washing over me. I wonder if it's hitting her as well. Though for Blake, I know it would be far more visceral and powerful. This place is just like the dank, dingy alley where they found Teresa Reyes.

This time though, the vic is Caucasian, with blonde hair and blue eyes that are wide open and staring at some fixed point beyond this world. Pretty girl, but with her short skirt that barely covers her intimate parts, a midriff-baring top, thigh-high stockings, and high heels trashy enough that they'd make a stripper blush, her profession isn't a question.

Blake is standing over her, staring down into the

girl's blue eyes, a dazed expression on her face. I can practically read the thoughts going through her mind, and her emotions are clearer to see than the clouds in the sky overhead.

"You all right?" I ask.

She nods. "I'm fine."

She squats down next to the body, studying the dead girl closely, her face a mask of focus and concentration. The hooker had her throat slit— just like Teresa Reyes. And also just like Teresa Reyes, she'd suffered a frenzy of stab wounds. There's so much blood and destruction of this woman's body; I can't even begin to count the number of wounds on her body. She's lying in a pool of dark, viscous blood, the whole scene looking like something out of some gory slasher flick.

"What do you see?" I ask, squatting down beside her.

"Overkill. A frenzied attack," she muses. "If I had to guess, I'd say he cut her throat from behind, then went to work on her. It's personal."

I nod. "Sounds right. And it's a show for us."

"Yeah, I had the same thought," she agrees. "Doubt we'll get a copy of the case file, so our observations are going to have to be good enough."

Standing up, I look around, and it doesn't take me long to find what it is I'm looking for: confirmation that this one is meant for us.

"On the dumpster," I point. "Lower right-hand corner."

Blake stands up and sighs. "Yeah, I see it."

"You tourists done yet?" Schreiber growls and walks over to us. "Can I do my freakin' job now?"

"I'm pretty sure you couldn't do your freakin' job before," I mutter.

"Always got a smart answer, don't you, Arrington?" he spits.

"It happens when you're smart," I reply. "Hence, your lack of—"

"Pax," Blake admonishes me. "Cut it out."

"You really should listen—"

Blake rounds on Schreiber. "And you can shut up too, Detective."

He actually does what she says and bites off his words. There aren't many people in this world who can get that guy to shut up. My respect for Blake just shot up another hundred points.

"Do you have an ID on the vic?" Blake asks.

"Melanie Woods," he replies grudgingly. "Twenty-seven. Obviously a hooker."

"Detective Sergeant Schreiber, you are dealing with a serial killer," she says.

"How do you figure?"

Blake points to the insignia painted on the dumpster. "That flaming cross has been painted at multiple crime scenes I've been investigating," she explains. "Either somewhere close to the body, or on the victim themselves."

"If that was true, why haven't I heard about it?" he

frowns. "Surely, somebody would have put it together before now."

"Look, I can't account for what did or didn't happen before. I'm telling you now though, that there are a lot of bodies on this guy," she says.

"She's not wrong, Schreiber," I add. "We have thirty-six confirmed cases all across the country. Thirty-seven now, including Melanie here."

"That's bull," he sneers. "If that was the case—"

"Forget about what should or shouldn't have happened. It's irrelevant at this point," I say. "All that matters is what we do right here, right now. And I'm telling you that we have a guy with a pile of bodies running around out there."

Schreiber turns to Blake. "If that's true, why hasn't the almighty FBI tracked this guy down yet? Why haven't they even acknowledged that a monster like this exists?" he says with a feral grin. "Oh right, I guess you guys are having enough problems of your own right now."

"Detective Schreiber—"

"I'll tell you what I see," he cuts her off. "I see one dead hooker, probably cut up by her john. And I see a bit of graffiti that for all we know, has been here for ten freakin' years. Could be the logo for some band for all I know."

"Top-notch police work," I roll my eyes. "As always."

"Now, if you two are done playing lookie-loo, I've

got actual work to do," he growls. "My good humor is done, as is my professional courtesy. Get off my crime scene."

Blake looks like she's going to argue further but seems to think better of it and storms away from the body instead. I shake my head.

"Look up the name Teresa Reyes, Schreiber. Compare the crime scene photos," I urge him. "Do your job."

"Hey thanks, Arrington," he sneers. "But when I want advice about how to be a detective, I'll ask an actual detective. Now get out of here."

I shake my head and turn away, following Blake out to the car. He's not going to look into any of it just to spite me, and out of his own ignorance and laziness. All he sees is a dead hooker, and that's good enough for him. Schreiber has no intention of going below the surface. It's part of the reason Hayes has been able to operate so freely for two decades— apathy and laziness on the part of the SPD and all the other local departments.

I jump into Blake's car and shut the door behind me. She doesn't say a word as she speeds away from the crime scene with a squeal of tires, her face a mask of rage.

I know just how she feels.

TWENTY

Arrington Investigations; Downtown Seattle

"That bastard," she seethes. "He's going to let people die because he won't do his job."

"Now you see why I punched him."

"I now wish you'd punched him a few more times," she growls.

We're sitting in my office after our trip to the crime scene. Brody swept the office earlier and didn't find any new surveillance equipment. His office and my office were the only ones that didn't have any bugs in them originally, but I had him sweep them anyway.

Blake takes a drink of her water and sits back in the chair, physically doing her best to calm herself down. She looks at me, and I can see the frustration in her face.

"I'm hoping that once he cools off, he'll do his job,"

she says. "I'm hoping he isn't going to sweep this under the rug just because he's got a hard on for you."

"Knowing Schreiber like I do, I'm pretty sure he's going to do the bare minimum," I sigh. "He just doesn't care. Hasn't as long as I've known him. To him, a dead hooker is a dead hooker, and doesn't deserve a lot of consideration."

Blake's face darkens, and she takes a drink, doing her best to control herself. She's furious. If she were less professional, she probably would have punched Schreiber herself. A few times.

"Okay, so we need to assume that we're not going to be getting any help from SPD," I start. "We're on our own."

"I agree," she says.

Blake sits up, seeming to finally have come back to herself. She puts the cap back on her water bottle and sets it aside as I watch the anger drain from her face. She ties her hair back, and just like that, the steely resolve I'm used to seeing from Blake is back. She's focused, and she's determined.

"Alright. So where do we start?" she asks.

"We need to figure out when his first kill was," I say. "And given the fact that his kill map covers a number of different states, it's going to be hard to pinpoint where it was."

Blake purses her lips, and I can see the wheels in her head turning, and I can tell she's got an idea. But I've known her long enough to know it's best to let her play this out on her own and to avoid pushing her. I take a drink of my coffee and give her a minute.

"Of the thirty-seven kills we know of, how many of them were in Washington?" she asks.

"Just the six you mentioned," I reply. "Why do you ask?"

She looks off into the distance, a faraway look on her face as she seems to be trying to figure something out in her head. Blake seems to have come to an answer and looks back at me.

"Read off the kills by state. Just the numbers," she says.

"What are you thinking?"

"Just do it," she orders. "Give me the breakdown by state."

"Okay, we've got the six here in Washington. Seven after today. We have sixteen in California, seven in Oregon," I say. "Three in New Mexico, three in Arizona, and one in Idaho."

She uncaps her water and takes another long swallow, processing all of the information I've just given her. But the raw numbers like that, with no context, don't mean much. Which means we need to give it some context.

"We need to set up a timeline," I say.

She nods. "We do."

"Okay, you do that, and I'll dig for more."

She arches her eyebrow at me. "You haven't deleted the back doors into the databases yet; I take it."

"Did you really think I would?"

She grins ruefully. "I suppose not."

For the next few hours, we work on our separate tasks. I use every trick I can think of to tease out more information, more potential victims, then study the crime scene photos carefully, searching for the flaming cross. And by the time we're done, I've found three more victims: two in Idaho, and one more in Oregon, bringing our running total to forty, including Melanie Woods.

Blake and I sit at the table, looking at the timeline she's put together on the whiteboard, and it's simply staggering to behold. Forty names. Forty lives snuffed out. The black and white photos and notes written on the board don't even convey the actual scope of what we're looking at. It doesn't do it justice. And for what? For one man's twisted sense of morality?

"It's monstrous," Blake whispers.

"To put it mildly."

As I stare at the board, at those forty names and the years they died, I feel the most profound sense of grief. I didn't know these people, but looking at the names on the board fills me with an overwhelming sense of loss. It feels like a fist made of ice punched its way through my chest, grabbed hold of my heart, and squeezed it so tight I can barely breathe. The last time I felt like this was when Veronica died.

"That look on your face right there?"

I look over at Blake, who's looking back at me pointedly. She points her finger at me to emphasize her point.

"That look on your face right there is proof, beyond the shadow of a doubt, that you are nothing like Hayes," she says. "That sorrow you're feeling, painted so clearly on your face right now, proves once and for all that you are capable of empathy and compassion. So next time you doubt yourself, remember this exact moment. You hear me?"

"Yeah, I hear you."

I give her a tight smile. I know that should make me feel better— and to some extent, it does. But at the same time, any sort of relief I derive from knowing I can finally put away those thoughts of being just like Hayes is immediately blunted by sorrow for those whose lives were snatched away and snuffed out by this absolute monster.

I sit up and push all thoughts from my mind. There will be time enough to unpack it all and analyze it later. Right now, we need to— I need to— put all of my focus and energy into catching the man who has taken forty lives. I take a long swallow of my coffee and sit back in my chair.

"So, what does the timeline tell us?" I ask.

"That so far as we know, he started killing in 1998," she replies.

"So far as we know. I don't believe for a moment that's it though," I say. "There could be cases not logged into the federal databases. You know how slow they can be to put the information in."

"Or cases where the cross wasn't flagged at all," she

notes. "Sloppy detectives miss things or are too lazy to do things the right way."

Who she's thinking of isn't a secret. She's right. I doubt the flaming cross will make it into Schreiber's case file at all. But that problem with laziness and apathy isn't limited to him alone. It's a problem with cops everywhere— and people in general. If there's a shortcut or a way to do less work, people will find it.

"Just because we don't have bodies that predate that, I don't believe there aren't more out there," she says.

I think back to my conversations with Hayes and recall his reaction when I told him we'd unearthed more than thirty of his kills. He hadn't had one. He'd asked me a question instead, deflecting my question neatly. And I'd been so focused on him and feeling that thrill of chasing the man; I'd let it slip by. I hadn't pressed him on it. I should have because, in retrospect, it occurs to me that was confirmation that there are indeed more out there.

The question is, how many? How many more names will we have on that whiteboard? How many more lives will have been snuffed out when this is all over?

"Okay, what do we know so far?" Blake asks. "Run down the profile you've been putting together for me."

I drum my fingers on the table as I order my thoughts. I've been working on putting a profile together, but I haven't fully locked in just yet. I'm unusually hesitant about it. Perhaps it's because as I look at the whiteboard, I see the enormity of it. I absolutely need to get this right. I see what's at stake in the starkest terms possible. If I'm wrong and we don't get this guy, we may need several more whiteboards before this is all said and done.

But if I don't lock it in and start searching for Hayes, our chances of nailing him are exactly zero. The profile isn't the end-all, be-all. It's a helpful tool and guidepost to help us on our way. It's a tool that can— and will— be amended as we go and collect more information to add to and refine it. It's a starting point. Nothing more.

"I think he's unassuming. Not the sort of guy who stands out in a room. He's a chameleon and can blend in anywhere," I say. "He got into the Morgans' house and this office without being seen."

"I agree. He's got to be completely nondescript," she replies. "And also good with camouflage."

"Exactly. He's also an omnivore. He kills men and women, regardless of age or ethnicity. Of his victims, twenty-three have been women, and sixteen men, so we know it's not specifically misogyny that drives him," I tell her. "We also know he believes he's on a crusade of his own design and uses religion as a prop—"

"Okay, stop right there," she says. "Why bring religion into this at all?"

"My guess is he believes he's exposing or highlighting the hypocrisy of organized religion. Remember, he has a special disdain for religion that probably formed in childhood," I say. "Also, maybe he gets off on the idea of cops spinning their wheels and questioning priests and pastors. Regardless, it muddies the waters enough that he can swim away undetected."

She thinks it over for a moment then nods. "Okay, that tracks."

I stand and pace the room as I speak, all of the disparate information in my head coalescing into one coherent profile. I stare at the whiteboard for a long moment as all of the random bits of information I have keep falling into place like I'm putting together one big mental jigsaw puzzle.

"We know he doesn't hold a traditional job. His murders are his work. His mission," I go on. "And we know he funds his lifestyle by targeting wealthy families and abducting their children. But his ransom demands are never exorbitant, and although it's a healthy chunk of money, it's not so much that the families will miss it much. It's always just enough to fund his lifestyle."

"Why do you think that is?" she asks.

A crooked grin splits my lips. "Because he believes that avarice is rude. Ill-mannered and endemic to those of lower character and those of lower birth. He believes it's a trait of the unwashed masses."

Blake nods. "I don't get the idea that he comes from money or of a particularly high birth though," she muses. "If he did, he likely wouldn't need to ransom kids for his lifestyle. But he also seems strangely obsessed with portraying himself as somebody who has. At least to you. That sort of need for you to know that he isn't of low birth just screams overcompensation for me."

"I agree with you. He's learned to mimic the behaviors and attitudes of the wealthy, but it's not natural to him."

"You would know," Blake cracks.

I chuckle. "This may be the one time I'm glad to have been raised the Arrington way, steeped in all of that pompousness and arrogance— I can spot the fakes and those who are putting on airs a mile away."

Blake and I share a laugh, but it soon fades away. The somberness of all those faces on the whiteboard staring back at us weighs heavily, saturating the air around us with solemnity and killing any good humor.

"It seems particularly important to him that you know he's of good character and a high birth," she says.

I think about it for a moment before the answer comes to me. "It's because I symbolize everything he wanted but never had growing up," I say. "Money, social standing, privilege... I got into all of the right schools, never wanted for anything, and had parents who loved me. In their own way, of course. I'm positive those are things he never had."

"And this goes back to what I said before. This isn't about you at all," Blake adds. "This all comes back to him. He's just focusing his attention on you because, in a way, he wants to be you."

"Exactly," I say with a nod. "He desperately wants to be part of high society and the privileged elite. Always has."

"This is good, Pax. This is really good," she says.

"It's a profile," I reply grimly. "But it's not going to bring this guy in."

"No, but it helps us keep whittling away at the haystack," she tells me. "We keep this up and soon enough, there won't be anything but the needle left."

I give her a faint smile. Patience has never been my strong suit. Rather than waxing philosophical and discussing the psychological underpinnings of this bastard, I'd rather be walking him into a cell right now. I just have to keep reminding myself that this is the job. It's a marathon, not a sprint. The profile is an important piece of the puzzle because if we can understand this guy, we have a better chance of catching him.

And the profile is solid. I turn it over and over in my head and look for the flaws and weak links in the chain but see none. Of course, this is simply based on the information we're working with right now. It's possible we receive new information that forces us to scrap the profile and build a new one. But as I look at the faces of the dead and see the way they all seem to be staring back at me, silently pinning their hope that I will bring them justice once and for all on me, I shudder. The enormity of the task before me feels like a physical weight pressing down on me. It's almost too much.

"Patience you must have, my young Padawan," Blake says as if reading my mind. "We'll get this guy."

"Yeah. We will," I nod, hoping I sound more confident than I feel.

TWENTY-ONE
REUBEN HAYES

Bainbridge Island

The night air is cool. A thick cover of clouds blots out the moonlight. A chill wind sweeps in off the Puget Sound, sending a cool shudder down my spine, but at the same time invigorating me. I hide behind the thick screen of bushes and watch the house, the echoes of their laughter still ringing in my ears. I see their faces, twisted with amusement, and hear their scornful words aimed at me.

I cut a glance around but don't see anybody on the street, nor any lights on in the houses. Other than the sound of a dog barking somewhere in the distance, all is quiet. All of these homes are spread out on large parcels of land, so even though they have neighbors, they aren't too close. Which is good. It lowers the odds of me being seen.

My stomach churns with excitement and fear and the pain of humiliation they made me feel. It all combines within me, making my insides feel as if they're on fire. I check my watch and see that it's three a.m. on the button. It's time. I take a deep breath, slide my gloves on, then pull down the ski mask and slip out of the bushes. Moving on light, swift feet, I follow the path that leads alongside the house, and into the backyard.

I try the sliding glass door on the back deck first. It slides open quietly. I smile beneath my mask. Figures. Rich people always think they're untouchable. I push the curtain aside and slip into the large room beyond. It's filled with all the trappings of wealth I expected to find. Ornate art on the walls. Plush furniture. Carefully curated décor. But I'm not here for that.

I move to the staircase and ascend to the second floor, taking care to avoid the creaking stairs I noted on my last trip into the house. I've carefully planned for this, doing my best to provide for every contingency. Sticking carefully to the side of the hall, avoiding the creaky boards in the middle, I make my way down the hall, careful to avoid bumping the pictures hanging on the walls.

The door at the end of the hall is halfway open. I can hear the soft sound of their breathing beyond. I slip into the room and see their forms beneath the covers on the bed. They're fellow teachers at the school I work at, but now they're just faceless shadows in the gloom. I swallow hard and give myself one last chance to back out of this. I can walk out of this house right now. No harm, no foul.

I reject the idea though. I have been wanting to do this for too long. I've felt it building inside of me; a darkness that's consumed me from the inside out. And I have a feeling— no, I am certain— that when I do this, I will be reborn. I'll no longer be the meek English teacher who lives hand to mouth, barely getting by, who can't get a date to save his life. I won't be the man women reject any longer because petty things like that will cease to matter to me.

I've felt this change brewing inside of me for a long time now. I've tried to push it away and ignore it. I've tried to deny it. But I'm meant for so much more. I'm meant for far greater things than being the poor preacher's kid from Kirkland. I have the ability to transcend my abusive childhood. To escape the near-poverty, I was forced to endure as my parents drank and smoked away their earnings from the church they founded.

The key to becoming, to transcending my past is right here before me. Delia Johnson and her sometimes boyfriend Alex Ellison are the key to unlocking everything inside of me. I see that now. I see they did me a favor when they mocked and tormented me when I made the mistake of asking Delia out.

I was completely unaware she had a boyfriend, but that didn't stop them from humiliating me in front of the rest of the faculty. And the bitter sting of rejection and humiliation they made me feel was every bit as vibrant as it had been when I was a kid. It brought back all of the sneering, mocking voices as loud and clear. As if I'd been suddenly transported back in time.

But this was more than mere pain of rejection. This was a sudden realization of the exact type of people they are. Fools. Charlatans. Sinners, if I were to use my father's bastardized term. They delight in harming others, and so I must remove them from this world.

Sliding the long-handled knife out of the sheath on my hip, I stand next to Alex's side of the bed and stare down at him. I'd expected to feel any number of things tonight; fear probably chief among them. But as I stand here, the blade of my knife hovering inches over Alex's throat like the Sword of Damocles itself, all I feel is calm. Certainty. I feel as if this is the first step on the road to becoming who and what I am meant to be.

As if he felt my standing beside him, even in sleep, Alex's eyes snap open. He stares at me with the starkest fear I've ever seen on another man's face. Without giving myself a moment to stop and think about what I'm doing, I act. His eyes grow impossibly wide as the point of the blade sinks into his throat. I force the knife down, carving through his soft flesh with glee. He lets out a wet gurgle as a thick, scarlet rivulet rolls from the corner of his mouth.

Alex spasms. The wet gurgle turns into a wet, choked cough. He sprays blood all over me. I revel in its warmth. Through the vibrations in the knife, I feel the muscles of his throat click, working overtime to save him. But they will not save him. I drive the knife deeper, burnished by my newfound purpose. Yes.

Delia gasps, falling out of the bed with a hard thump. I give the knife in Alex's throat a final, vicious twist and then yank it out of his flesh and sigh in contentment at the sound of rending flesh.

I come around the bed to find Delia pressed into the corner, her knees drawn up and her arms wrapped around herself. Tears stream down her face. The only sound coming from her is a choked sob. But then she turns and sees her boyfriend, the erstwhile Alex Ellison, and her eyes grow comically wide. A high, reedy keening sound passes her lips as she tears her eyes away from him and focuses on me again. More specifically, on the bloody knife in my hand.

"P—please don't hurt me," she cries.

Looming over her, I feel my own power growing. My transformation has begun. I am becoming.

"I should thank you," I say.

Her mouth drops open, and she looks at me, a tiny glimmering thread of curiosity wrapped around the ball of fear in her face.

"A—Alvin?" she stammers. "Is that you?"

I lean down and turn the lamp on her nightstand on, bathing the room in its soft, warm glow. My eyes still fixed on her, I slip off the mask, revealing the face she's accustomed to. She can't yet see the face that's growing beneath the surface. And she won't. That face will not be revealed until I finish this. Until I allow

Delia's blood— her sacrifice— to complete my metamorphosis.

I shall be baptized in her blood and come forth sanctified and pure. Yes.

Her eyes widen. The light from her lamp glitters off the tears rolling down her cheeks like chips of diamonds. She opens her mouth and closes it several times, looking like a fish out of water. Her entire body is trembling in fear. She has lost all control of herself.

"W—why are you doing this?" she gasps.

I inhale deeply, savoring the scent of her fear. I take one step forward. Then another.

She screams, but I reach my hand forcefully down and grab her by the throat, pinning her to the corner of the wall. Not enough for her to choke. Merely to stop her from running.

Whatever slight hope she may have had for escape is now snuffed out. Gone, like the life of Alex Ellison. Like her own life, in mere moments.

In a way, like the former life I had led. No longer shall I be bound by the fleeting morality of the world. I know my purpose. All that is left is to complete my becoming.

"Because of you— and Alex of course— I know my purpose," I whisper, my smile bright. "The pain and humiliation the both of you inflicted upon me was the exact key I needed to turn the lock inside of me."

She cries and shudders in my grasp. Her cries have given way to hysterics. I can feel her heartbeat skittering wildly in my palm. With every frantic beat of her pulse, I feel as if her life is leaving her and flowing into me. Yes.

"I—I—I don't know what—what—you're talking about. P-p-p-lease Alvin."

"If you hadn't rejected me, tormented, and humiliated me, I might have never known what I was capable of," I say. "I might never have found my purpose. To cleanse this world of tormenters and betrayers. To purify it. Without you, I may have never had the strength or courage to transform into what I was always meant to be."

"P-p-please Alvin."

I look down at her and smile. Her beauty strikes me as hard today as it did the day I first laid eyes on her. And her role in helping me to ascend, to transform, only makes her more beautiful in my eyes.

"Thank you, Delia," I say. "You will always be special to me. Very special."

Yes.

I breathe deeply, savoring the scent of the Sound. I toast the clear evening air and take a sip of a very fine *Chateau Cheval Blanc* Bordeaux, rolling it around my tongue before I swallow. A sound of extreme pleasure and delight passes my lips. The wine warms and soothes me with an intoxication just as deep as the memory.

That was October twenty-third, 1996. Delia and Alex were my first, though I treasure the memory of her more than him for obvious reasons. I loved her. Wanted her. And as I accepted her sacrifice and started to transform into what I am today, I shared something special with her. It is an intimacy I've never experienced with another person before in my life, and one I doubt I ever will again. That bond I shared with Delia that night will forever be in my heart.

There are moments in time when I am agitated or anxious that I think about her and that night, that special intimacy we shared, and it calms me down. It soothes me in ways not even a good eighties power ballad can. As I transformed into this new life, I rediscovered my love and passion for music. Specifically, the music of my youth kindled a sense of nostalgia within me that never fails to make me smile.

Hearing those songs I loved as a child again helped me find those few good memories from my childhood and hold onto them. For so long, my soul was filled with nothing but darkness. Hatred. Bitterness. And anger. But once I transformed, once I was baptized by Delia's sacrifice, it cleansed my soul. It was suddenly as new and fresh as the day I was born.

So I filled it with music. Memories. I filled my soul with the happier things I managed to find from my previous life and even started to build new memories. And of course, my purpose. My mission. None of those things would have been possible without Delia's sacrifice. Without her contribution to my metamorphosis. And for that reason, she will always hold a very special place in my heart.

"To you, Delia," I say, and take another drink.

As I look out at the water, watch the boats that cross the Sound, leaving trails of white in their wake, my mind turns outward again, and I focus on what's before me. Paxton's discovery of the surveillance equipment I'd planted in his office was an inconvenience, to be sure. But it also raised the esteem I hold him in even higher. I have no idea how he figured it out, but it is exciting. It shows me that I'm right about him.

But it left me with a blind spot. I needed to know what they know and what they're seeing. So as much as I do not like to kill so close to home, I was forced to. I knew that marking a body I've cleansed with the symbol they would recognize would bring them running. And sure enough, it did. Just as I knew it would.

I used the opportunity while they were distracted to plant another mic in Agent Wilder's satchel. I knew they would return to Paxton's office, and so they did. And I listened in on their entire conversation about me, impressed with just how thorough and insightful Paxton is. His profile of me, though difficult to listen to at certain points, is more or less dead on. It shows me that I am right. He is truly meant to build upon my legacy.

All I must do is get Agent Wilder out of the way so he can see that. She keeps undoing all the work I've been doing to prepare him for his own becoming. I have been working hard to lay the groundwork for his metamorphosis, only to have that woman interfere and undo everything I've done.

She has become a distraction. A nuisance to be dealt with. And fortunately, she may also be the key Paxton needs to unlock that door inside of him. The door that leads to his own becoming.

TWENTY-TWO

PAXTON

Arrington Investigations; Downtown Seattle

"Jesus, that's a lot of names," Brody gasps.

I nod. "Sure is."

"And you're absolutely sure that one guy did all this?"

I nod again. "As sure as I am that your name is Brody."

I sit at the table in the conference room, going over all of my notes and the case files I do have. It's been a few days since the Melanie Woods murder, and Blake hasn't heard word one from Schreiber. Not that either of us are surprised. I'm tempted to give Deputy Chief Torres a call and have him come down here to look at my whiteboard, but he'll tell me what Blake's superiors keep telling her— the evidence is flimsy, and they won't use resources they don't have on what could be a wild goose chase.

And after some introspection and careful thought, I suppose I can't really blame them all too much. I hate that I can't, but I really can't. Other than the flaming cross, there is no direct evidence linking all of these murders together. Hayes is amazingly good at covering his tracks and using forensic countermeasures to keep people guessing. He varies his methods just slightly enough so that patterns can't be established, and he chooses victims with exacting specifications. He has honed his craft over the past two decades to be nearly unpredictable.

And it's my job to predict where he'll strike next. Before it's too late.

Torres won't take my word that I've spoken to the killer and that he's claimed credit for all forty bodies—and more if we ever find them. And rather than bite the bullet, take some heat, and open a full and public investigation into the killer, both the SPD and the Bureau are simply tucking their heads into the sand and playing the cover-your-butt game. See no evil, hear no evil, speak no evil.

But evil will continue slaughtering innocents until it's stopped.

"Jesus," Brody mutters again, his voice tinged with awe.

"And nobody is looking for this guy, let alone trying to stop him," I say, my voice thick with frustration.

"And this guy was in this office?" Brody asks, a nervous tremor in his voice.

"He was," I reply.

"I may need to work from home for a while. I'm not built to deal well with genocidal maniacs."

I give him a wry smile. "I think he needs to kill several thousand more before he qualifies as genocidal."

Brody shrugs. "You said you don't know how many this guy has killed," he points out. "For all you know, there's a giant pit out there somewhere with fifty thousand bodies in it. I think that would surely qualify."

A grim laugh escapes me. It's melodramatic and unlikely, but he's not entirely wrong. We just don't know how many bodies are out there, and we won't until we have Hayes in our custody. Once we do though, I think we'll find out the full scope of his monstrous life. Knowing him as I do, I'm sure he won't be able to resist telling me how many people he's killed.

He'll tell me not only as a point of pride but also because he thinks he'll be showing me the full breadth of his good works in this world. He'll want to show me how much of a difference he's made in cleansing the world of the impure and sinful. He'll try to convince me once more that his work is necessary, and that because we are so similar, I should be the one to pick up his mantle and carry on with his work.

But as I stare at the faces on the whiteboard, I'm struck once more by how much I'm not like him. And I can't believe I ever entertained the notion. I realize the darkness that exists within me is born not of a homicidal urge, but something else. Something far more mundane and personal. Although I once toyed with the idea of whether or not I could do what Hayes is doing, I know beyond the shadow of a doubt now, that I could not. And those were the thoughts of an immature, selfish, self-absorbed mind.

The change Veronica wrought in me was not pulling me from the edge of that darkness, but in showing me that light exists within me. She opened my eyes to the world around me. She showed me that for far too long, I lived inside my own mind, never feeling at home in high society and the Arrington way of life, but never being a part of the 'common folk' either.

She showed me that I existed between two worlds, with a foot in neither, so I retreated inward. And if you exist in that in-between space in your own mind for too long, of course, your thoughts will turn dark. You will become bitter and angry. My darkness was simply a product of my own retreat inward and self-absorption.

It's why I cling so hard to a life of service. Of helping others. It has brought me out of that darkness and into the light. And the years I spent sharing that light with Veronica were the best of my life. So in keeping her memory alive, I'm also keeping myself alive. As long as I'm living a life I know Veronica would be proud of, I can keep myself in the light. Living a life of service and keeping her alive in my heart is as much about me as it is her.

Call that selfish if you want. I call it necessary. I don't want to go back to being the person I was before I met Veronica. That's what my family—my parents in particular—don't understand. And I don't even think Blake fully gets it either. But I do and I know Veronica does, and in the end, that's all that matters.

"You all right, man?" Brody asks.

I nod. "I was just thinking about how all of this has helped me understand myself in ways I haven't since Veronica died."

"What do you mean?"

"Just that I enjoy living in the light rather than in the darkness."

"Vague and ominous-sounding, but okay."

I laugh. "It makes sense to me."

"And that's all that matters."

"Just what I was thinking."

We share a moment of companionable silence, and Brody lays his hand on my shoulder, giving it a gentle squeeze.

"You're gonna catch this guy, Pax. I know you can. And I'm with you every step of the way."

I look up at him and hold his gaze. "Thanks."

TWENTY-THREE
REUBEN HAYES

Nelson's Supermarket; Downtown Seattle

"Thank you very much," I say. "And have yourself a very pleasant evening."

"You too, sir," the cashier replies.

I catch sight of her from the corner of my eyes as I push my cart away from the register and head for the door, making a show of my limping and near immobility. I'm just another octogenarian out buying groceries at eight at night, don't mind me.

Thanks to the tracker I placed under the rear bumper of Special Agent Wilder's car the same day I dropped the bug into her satchel, I am able to find her at a moment's notice. I followed her from the FBI field office to Pike Place, and now into a supermarket for a few things.

Judging by her groceries, it looks like she is planning

on making dinner for somebody. I can't help but wonder if it's Paxton. Perhaps I was wrong, and she's not the Irene Adler in his life after all. The mutual respect is definitely there between them, but perhaps it's not platonic, and she's actually his paramour.

If that's the case, I must say they hide it very well. I see the chemistry between them, but to me, it seems as if they really are nothing more than friends. That gives me even more reason to take Special Agent Wilder off the board. I do not want, nor need, Paxton to be distracted. I want him laser focused and... well, if I'm being honest, I want him vulnerable.

I've found that people who are vulnerable and going through a crisis are so much more malleable. It will be far easier to mold and shape him, to help him see his true potential and what he is capable of being, if Special Agent Wilder is no longer in the way, twisting his mind in ways that run counter to my instruction and guidance.

But to get him to do what I want him to do, to help open his eyes to what he's truly capable of being, I need to give him the one thing he wants above all else. Answers about his wife. I know he's been digging into her death ever since she died. I know he doubts the official story. And I know he's not getting the answers he so desperately wants.

It's the one thing I can offer him that will get him to do what I want and need him to do, which is to open his eyes and see himself for what he truly is. It's the one thing that will bring him to my way of thinking and let him see that, like me, he can ascend. Transform. And join me in my work to cleanse this world.

I've parked two cars down from Agent Wilder's car and am still fumbling with my keys when she comes out of the store. By the time she reaches her car, I have my trunk open and put the first bag in. But then I stumble and drop my second bag, falling to the ground heavily in the process. I groan loudly like it's the worst pain I've felt in my life.

Agent Wilder is there in the blink of an eye, hovering over me, a look of genuine compassion and concern in her face.

"Very Johnny on the spot of you, Special Agent Wilder."

As I smile, I see her expression changing from one of concern to one of fear tinged with anger as the realization that she's been had dawns on her. She reaches for the holster on her hip, but she's too late. I bring out the stun gun I'd concealed in my sweater and press it to her skin. And as I pull the trigger and watch her start to twitch, I smile.

I quickly get to my feet and zap her again just to be sure. As she lies on the ground, groaning and writhing, I look around but am gratified to see there's nobody out at this hour. I pick her up and drop her into my trunk; then, after taking her service weapon, I bind her wrists and ankles with zip ties. With her secured, I inject her with a sedative that should ensure she remains out cold until we return home.

I watch her for a moment as the sedative begins to take hold. Her eyes flutter, and her body starts to grow limp. It's not long before her eyes close, and she starts the deep, even breaths of sleep. That done, I close the trunk lid.

"That was disappointingly easy, Special Agent Wilder," I muse. "Paxton would not have made such a clumsy error."

Grinning to myself, I get behind the wheel and drive off into the night with my prize. And my test for Paxton. If he passes, he will come through it a changed man. He'll have proved his worth to build upon my legacy, and we can begin doing great things together. We can begin cleansing the stains of humanity off the fabric of this world.

But, if he fails, I'll have to kill him. Which would be truly disappointing.

TWENTY-FOUR

PAXTON

Arrington Investigations; Downtown Seattle

When I get Blake's voicemail— again— I disconnect the call and drop the phone onto my desk, the slight concern that had blossomed yesterday, blooming into outright worry today. It's been two days since I last spoke with Blake. She's not returning my calls or text messages. I've even left several messages at her office. All to no avail.

I know she's got a lot going on. In addition to the Hayes case, she's been assigned to look into several other cases at the same time. I imagine her superiors are trying to bury her in other work to divide her attention with the hope she'll drop it entirely to focus on current cases instead.

But they obviously don't know Blake like I do. She's a bulldog. Once she gets her teeth into something, she does not let it go. And her teeth are fully sunk into the Hayes case. She is one hundred percent engaged with it, and knowing her as I do, she would never simply walk away. Especially without mentioning something to me about it first. She would have at least given me a heads up.

Which makes her sudden radio silence all the more worrisome. The only reason I can think of for her going dark like this is that she's been thrown into some undercover assignment and can't contact me. But I can't imagine some deep undercover case popping up this quickly. They would not just throw her in unprepared for something like that. Not even the idiots over at SPD would do that. Undercover work takes some time and prep work.

Brody comes through my office door with his tablet and a grim look on his face. It sends a cold chill slithering down my spine. The thought of anything happening to Blake makes my stomach churn, and my heart threatens to stop dead in my chest.

"What is it?" I ask. "What did you find?"

"It's not what I found, man. It's what the SPD found," he says. "And they found Blake's car outside Nelson's. It's been in the parking lot of a couple of days."

I'm on my feet before I'm even aware I've moved. A greasy, nauseous feeling wells up in my gut, and my heart starts to beat harder than if I'd just run a marathon. I take the tablet from Brody and scan through what he's found. Which is nothing other than Blake's car. The groceries were in the back seat along with her satchel, and they found a tracking device under the rear bumper. There's only one person who could have done this... Hayes. He's been stalking her. On the positive side though, they thankfully found no blood and most importantly, no body.

There's no question in my mind about who did this. Who took her. The fact that he'd flaunted that he'd known about her should have tipped me off. I should have known. He wouldn't have mentioned that he knew about Blake unless he wanted me to know. And the only reason he'd want me to know is that he planned to use her to draw me into his stupid game.

Brody looks at me, his expression as sober as I've ever seen it. "You don't think—"

"No," I cut him off and shake my head. "No. She's alive. If Hayes was going to kill her, we'd have found the body by now."

"Then why did he take her?"

"It's all part of his game," I say softly. "She has some part to play in all of this. He's using her to get to me."

Just saying the words, knowing how true they are, hits me like a sledgehammer to the gut. I have to sit down again. My legs suddenly feel weak, and I'm having a hard time catching my breath. Knowing that Blake is in danger because of me— because of this freak's fascination with me— turns my stomach.

But it also makes me angry. I'm filled with a seething

rage that lights up every cell in my body. He's crossed a line. This just makes me more determined than ever to find this man and put a stop to his madness. I don't care if I have to kill him myself to do it. This sick psycho is going down. For good.

My mind is spinning. I'm trying to figure out what my next move is going to be when my phone rings. Brody and I exchange a look, then I snatch up my phone, see it's from a blocked number, and connect the call.

"Where is she?" I roar.

"Tsk tsk," he says. "You really should learn proper phone etiquette."

"Where— is— she?" I growl. "What have you done with her?"

"Imagine if I had been a telemarketer. Or a client," he replies, a laugh in his voice. "That might have been embarrassing for you."

"Screw you, Hayes," I spit. "Tell me where she is."

"You of all people should know how seriously I take manners, Paxton," he says. "I abhor boorish behavior."

"I swear to God, if you don't—"

"I also do not tolerate threats," he cuts me off, his voice suddenly cold. "Now, if you cannot control yourself and show me some proper courtesy and respect, I will hang up now and you will never see Special Agent Wilder again. At least, not until she turns up in the city morgue. Are we clear?"

I draw a deep breath and swallow down the anger

coursing through every vein in my body. I want nothing more than to crush this man's skull, but he's right. I need to control myself. I know better than anybody that he demands manners and courtesy. If I have any hope of getting Blake out of this mess, I'm going to have to play by his rules. I cut a glance at Brody, who gives me an encouraging nod.

"We're clear," I sigh, injecting as much civility into my tone as possible. Which, at the moment, is not much.

"That will do, I suppose."

"Where is she, and why have you taken her?" I ask.

"To answer your first question, all in due time," he says. "As to the second, it is to help you become who you were meant to be."

"And who was I meant to be? Your protege?"

"If it helps you to see yourself in that role, so be it," he replies. "But I see you as more of a kindred spirit, Paxton. You know how important the work I'm doing is. I've heard you speak about what a blight on the world people can be. Surely you understand what it is I'm doing."

My mind flashes to the forty faces on the whiteboard in the conference room, and anger wells up within me once more. I have to physically fight to keep it from boiling over. Seeing me on the verge of blowing up again, Brody gives me a 'calm down' gesture.

"What is it you want from me, Hayes?"

"I want you to ascend," he says. "Like me, I want

you to transform yourself and thus, help transform this world."

I realize at this point, I can stand here and bicker with him, which doesn't put me a single step closer to saving Blake. Or I can play along with him and pick the best opportunity to take this guy out. But I know I have to play it right. I can't sit here and pretend to be all in, or he'll know I'm faking it. I have to be the reluctant dupe.

"What is it going to take for me to get Blake out of there and to safety?" I ask.

"Find her. All you have to do is find her," he says.

"And how am I going to do that?"

"By finding me, of course," he says, then lets out that creepy giggle of his.

I cut a glance at Brody, who looks as dismayed by it as I do. I turn back to the phone and shake my head, wanting nothing more than to reach through the phone and strangle him.

"You realize how circular that logic is, don't you?" I ask.

"Round and round," he sings. Another eighties tune. "What comes around goes around."

Brody looks at me with wide eyes, his expression saying this is the most bizarre thing he's ever heard. He's not wrong. For as intelligent and cunning as this guy is, he's also got more than a few screws loose.

"It's not as circular as you might think," Hayes says. "If you find me, you will find her."

"Great," I mutter. "Text me with an address and I'll Google Map it now."

"There it is. There's the lighthearted banter I was missing." I can practically hear him beaming through the phone, and it takes all I have not to crush it in my hands. "Glad to have you back, Paxton."

I roll my eyes and blow out a frustrated breath. "If you're not going to give me an address, how am I supposed to find you?"

"Oh Paxton, do not disappoint me. I know you're smarter than that," he says. "You already have everything you need to know to find me. You just need to put on your deerstalker cap, grab a pipe, and put that big brain of yours to use."

"This isn't a book, and I'm not Sherlock Holmes."

"Don't I know it?" he titters again. "Sherlock would never be as dim as you're being right now. But then, you probably already know that."

"I already have everything I need to know?" I ask. "What are you talking about? I don't have—"

"Daylight is burning, Paxton. You have until midnight tonight to crack the code. I want you to tell me the name of my very first kill," he says. "Midnight, Paxton. And you know how I feel about punctuality. If you are not able to give me the name of my first kill by midnight, I am afraid we will all have to bid sayonara to Special Agent Wilder."

"Wait. Just wait," I demand. "Prove to me she's still alive. Let me talk to her."

"You know that I am a man of my word."

"I also know you kidnap children for a living," I respond. "And you kill others for fun."

"No, no, no!" he roars. "I cleanse this world of the stains of humanity."

"If that's what you need to tell yourself, fine by me. I'm not going to argue with you," I tell him. "But I also won't be doing anything you ask until you let me speak with Blake."

He lets out a frustrated breath. "Fine."

There's a shuffling sound and the distant echo of voices. A moment later, I'm hit with a wave of relief deeper and more profound than anything I've ever felt before.

"Don't play his game, Pax," comes Blake's voice, slurred and weak. "Don't do it."

"Blake," I gasp. "I'm going to get you out of this. I swear it—"

"Don't, Pax—"

Her voice is cut off and is quickly replaced by Hayes'. "Happy?"

"Why does she sound like you drugged her?"

"Well, because I did," he replies. "I had to keep her compliant."

"Hayes, I swear—"

"What did I tell you about making threats?" he snaps back. "And don't worry, she will be fine. It's just a sedative."

"Look, what if I come to you on my own. You can let her go and—"

"That will not work," he interrupts. "No cops. No FBI. Just you and your big brain, Arrington. If you call them, I will know, and that will be the end. No, I need you to prove yourself to me. To prove you are worthy."

It seems like I've been trying to prove myself to somebody all my life. First my father, and now to Hayes. I miss those days when I was with Veronica. When I didn't have to prove myself to anybody. I could just be free.

"Fine," I say. "Just tell me—"

"As I said, you have everything you need to find me already," he says. "Apply yourself. Show me you are who I think you are. Become the person you were always meant to become, Paxton. Just... do it by midnight."

The line goes dead in my hand. I let out a roar of rage that makes Brody look like he's about to jump out of his skin. I turn and hurl the phone against the plexiglass wall of my office, leaving a small scuff on it, but shattering the phone into a million pieces.

Brody stares at the remnants of the phone lying scattered all over the floor of my office. He purses his lips and nods. "Okay well, I think I'm going to need to go and replace that."

Brody turns and heads for the elevators without another word. He's about as non-confrontational of a guy as you're going to find anywhere. He's not too keen on big displays of emotion like that. I'll have to apologize to him when he gets back. If he gets back. He may stay away for an hour or two just to give me a minute to calm down. Which isn't exactly a bad idea.

It's a good thing I have a spare phone.

TWENTY-FIVE

Arrington Investigations; Downtown Seattle

I walk out of my office and into the conference room, dropping down into one of the chairs heavily. I check my backup phone and see that it's eight forty-six in the morning. Which means I've got fifteen hours and fourteen minutes to crack the code and figure out where he's holding Blake.

I stare at the whiteboard, trying to decipher the tangled mess in front of me. Photographic evidence of human depravity. Of one man's delusions and self-absorption. Hayes has appointed himself judge, jury, and executioner. The sole arbiter of what is good and what is right. Of what is moral and what is immoral. He's decided to declare himself a god, deciding who gets to live and who must die based on nothing more than his personal interpretation of morality.

I scrub my face with my hands and growl. All of these observations are great and all, but they get me no closer to finding him. To finding Blake.

"Think, idiot," I growl at myself. "Think."

I stand up and pace the conference room, looking at the board from different angles and distances. I stand on chairs, on the table, even going outside the conference room to stare in at the whiteboard from the other side of the glass. I don't know if physically giving myself a different perspective will give me an actual different perspective, but at this point, I'm willing to try anything.

What I need right now is Blake. She never has a problem thinking outside the box and figuring out a different way of attacking a situation. I am sometimes far too linear in my thinking. I lack the creativity Blake's got in spades. It's why we've made such a great team. Muttering darkly under my breath, I walk back into the conference room and perch on the edge of the table, staring at the board, trying to will the answer to come forth.

"I have everything I need to find him," I repeat his words. "It's all right here."

I stare at the pictures, the names, the stacks of paper, and case files. The answer is here somewhere; I just need to find a different way of looking at it all to tease it out. I clear the table and pick out all of the crime scene photos, laying them all out in one large grid for me to look at. Once I get them all laid out, I step back and fold my arms over my chest and look at the photos, taking a moment to study them all.

At first, all I see are the torn, broken bodies. Nothing but blood, gore, and violence. But as I force myself to continue staring at the photos, I start to see past the slasher film quality of them and start to pick out details. Small details at first: the broken glass on the ground, the rusted tin can, or the corroded hole in the dumpster behind the body.

And it's as the fine details begin to emerge that I start to see things differently. I imagine this is what Blake must see and feel like all the time. She sees the fine details without even having to try. It's second nature to her. And because she can, she can let her mind think creatively, to see things outside the normal way of thinking. It's how I imagine she's able to think so effectively outside the conventional box.

I free my mind and let it take the lead. Instead of trying to think, trying to see, I let my subconscious do the work for me. And it immediately zeroes in on the flaming cross. No matter what else I look at, my mind comes back to the religious iconography. His trademark.

There is no specific religious angle to the murders. Despite his proclamations of purity and sin and cleansing, Hayes is not a religious man. It is a symbol he uses to mark his work, but it carries no specific spiritual meaning for him personally. When I questioned him about it, he played it off. He moved on from it quickly.

And as I replay the conversation in my mind, I see that maybe he played it off too quickly.

At the time, I backed off the questioning because I wanted to keep him talking, and I feared he was on the verge of clamming up. And after that, I didn't give it much thought. He obviously harbored some ill will for organized religion, but I wrote it off as childhood trauma. Some sort of angst or dislike that developed when he was young.

At the time, I posited that he grew up in a religious family and didn't have a very good experience. I can't count the number of people for whom that is true. Bad experiences with something when you're young, whether it's religion, scary movies, or even clowns, can inform your biases and prejudices toward those things later in life. I think that's true in almost every case. Something you viscerally dislike as an adult can often be traced back to some relatively traumatic experience with it when you were young.

But now, my mind is forcing me to take another look at it. To see it differently. Although Hayes said there's no relevance to the iconography, that doesn't mean there's not. I shouldn't have taken him at his word and should have explored this angle further earlier on. Maybe if I had, Melanie Woods would still be alive and Blake—

"No. Knock it off," I growl at myself. "Stop thinking that way. It's counterproductive, and there's no way of knowing whether or not it's true."

Grabbing my phone, I take a picture of the flaming cross and send it to my email account, then walk back to my office. I download the picture, call up the search engine, and do a reverse image search. As the computer works, I silently chastise myself once more for not thinking of doing this earlier. This should have been step number one.

"Rookie mistake," I mutter.

The search results come up, and I stare at all of the different links that come up. News articles, blog posts, various other internet trash. I start to click through the links, reading quickly, and absorbing all of the information I'm taking in.

All of the pieces I've read so far reference a single place that uses that specific symbol: The Everlasting Fire of Christ Church, based just outside of Kirkland, WA. I read on through some of the different pieces. Most of them paint a very bleak picture of the EFCC, as they call it. Well, most people call it something more vulgar, but I'll stick with the EFCC.

Most of the pieces I'm reading are newspaper articles from the digital archives of local papers. To say they're unflattering would be an understatement. Most charge it with being on par with the grifting snake-oil salesmen of faith healing churches. Others go so far as to label it a cult, characterizations that hold true to some blog posts and newspaper articles from more recent times.

I finally find an actual informational article about

them and read closely. The EFCC has been around since the late 70's and was founded by a husband and wife team, Jacob and Karen Perry. From what I'm gathering, back then, it was more of a free-love hippie commune than an actual religious outfit. People would come to the farm to live and pray and smoke weed all day, discussing all things metaphysical and philosophical. Some stayed on and lived there.

According to some of the stories, the only true religious experiences in those early days came in the form of communing with God during an acid trip. Sounds like the First Church of Timothy Leary to me.

Over the years, though, the EFCC has changed its reputation, moving away from what it was founded as, to more of a holy-rolling fundamentalist group steeped in big flashy shows of faith. Some people view the EFCC as a group of doomsday preppers, all of them waiting for the end of days. Others see them as another group like the Branch Davidians, arming themselves to the teeth to defend their freedom from what they see as an oppressive, anti-religious government. And still, others view them as a cult using the guise of religion to mask their depravity behind their tax-exempt status.

There really is no consensus about the EFCC, what they are, or what they stand for. Which tells me the EFCC's biggest crime is that they're different. And people tend to reject those things that are different. Always labeling them and judging them harshly. It may be true, some of the things people are saying. But in my experience, the people who are the loudest in decrying this group or that group are the people who know the least about them. And the Internet is a place built for people to be loud.

What I don't see, though, is any mention of the Perrys themselves. I don't see any follow-up articles about where they went or what became of them. At some point in the late eighties, it seems, they just vanished without a trace. At least their online footprint vanished without a trace. If they really are old hippies, they could be living out their golden years the same way they lived their life: off the grid.

That symbol is important to Hayes. Important enough for him to use it as his calling card. The biggest question I have is whether or not it's important because he belonged to the EFCC at some point— which might jibe with his anger toward religion— or whether he simply liked the look of their symbol and co-opted it for his own purposes.

This is good. This potentially opens up a lot of areas of inquiry. Or it could be a dead end. Either way, it raises a lot of questions. And there's only one way to get the answers.

"Guess I'm going to Kirkland."

TWENTY-SIX

Everlasting Fire of Christ Church; Kirkland, WA

I pull into the gravel parking lot, listening to the small stones crunch beneath my tires as others plunk the inside of the wheel well. There are half a dozen other cars in the lot. I shut my engine off and sit back, taking it all in for a moment.

The EFCC is tucked away on a small farm on the outskirts of Kirkland. The place looks to be much the same as when the church bought it all those years ago. It's large and open. I see what look to be apple orchards in the distance, along with rows and rows of crops as well. Surprisingly, in one fenced-off section near the parking lot, I see rows of solar panels.

Off to the western side of the property is what looks like a farmhouse. It's tall, and the paint looks fresh as if it's been done in the last few weeks. It's very well kept up, even more so than the other buildings on the property. I'm assuming it's because that serves as the hub for their church.

    The farmhouse itself looks old fashioned. It's three stories tall, painted white with green trim and shutters. There are some outbuildings beyond the main farmhouse. Bungalow style houses. Everything is neat and clean, buildings and fences are all in good repair, and there's an air of freshness about the place.

    Far from being a compound that houses a secret cult or some anti-government militia, it looks like a self-sustaining group of people who prefer to live off the grid, in their own way. These people look like they've opted to eschew the high-tech conveniences of the modern world— and all of its problems— in favor of a simpler world. A simpler life. And as I look around, soaking in the peace and tranquility of the place, I can see the appeal.

    I make my way over to the farmhouse, and it's there that I see it. Emblazoned on the front of the church, twenty feet tall, twenty feet wide: the flaming cross Hayes uses to tag his murders.

    I stare at it for a long moment and feel a peculiar sense of rightness wash over me. It's thick and strong, and as I look at the logo on the barn, I know beyond a reasonable doubt that I'm going to find some answers here. I know it as well as I know my own name. They may not be the direct answers to my questions, and they may not be answers I was expecting, but I'm going to get some answers. I can feel it.

I get out of my car and step into the cold air of the day. The sky overhead is slate gray, and a light mist falls from the clouds. A group of people are clustered together near the barn. They're all looking at me with open curiosity. I straighten my jacket and walk toward them, watching them smile as I approach.

A tall, broad-shouldered young man with dark hair and eyes steps forward, a welcoming expression on his face. He's dressed in modern enough clothing— blue jeans, a dark hoodie, and a new pair of Nikes on his feet. So they apparently don't eschew all of the modern world's niceties. I can't begrudge them that though. Who wants to wear wool pants you made yourself?

"Welcome, brother. Welcome to the Everlasting Fire of Christ Church," he greets me warmly. "I don't believe I've seen you at fellowship before."

"That would be because I haven't been to fellowship before," I reply with a grin.

"A newcomer. Wonderful. We love having new faces join us for worship."

I have to admit; I'm surprised by how open and friendly they are. When I was reading about them online, I actually did expect either paper robe-wearing zealots preaching about their alien overlords or grizzled men with an arsenal of guns drawing down on me. Seeing the EFCC live and in-person is making me realize my own biases and ignorance. I'm not nearly as open-minded as I've always thought. I obviously have much to learn still.

"Actually, I was hoping to speak with the pastor here," I say. "Would that be Jacob and Karen Perry?"

He cocks his head and looks at me. "Oh, heavens no," he says. "I'm David Miller. My father, Aaron, is the pastor and leader of the EFCC. Who are Jacob and Karen Perry?"

"Probably before your time," I reply with a small smile. "Is your father around? I'd like to speak with him."

"Of course. He's in the chapel," David says. "Follow me."

I follow him into the barn and appreciate the way it's been converted into a church. Everything is clean and polished, the hardwood floors and pews sparkling in the light. Tapestries bearing symbols, inspirational quotes, and Bible passages hang from the loft and are mounted on the walls, and over to the right is what looks like a coffee area. Like The Pulpit, the EFCC has repurposed everything and turned it into a warm, welcoming place. I can't help but admire it.

There is an older man standing at the front of their chapel, just below a massive wooden carving of the cross and flame taking up nearly the whole wall. He's down on his hands and knees, polishing the wood dais by hand to a glossy shine. He looks up as we approach and gets to his feet, wiping his hands on his rag, a warm smile on his face. He's wearing a dark coverall with a white t-shirt beneath, and a red bandana wrapped around his neck. Not exactly the garb I'm used to seeing on a preacher.

"Who's your friend, David?"

The younger man turns to me. "You know? I never did catch your name."

"Sorry," I say. "I'm Paxton."

"Well Paxton, it's nice to meet you. I'm Aaron Miller," he greets me with a strong handshake.

"It's nice to meet you, sir," I nod.

"I'll leave you two to it then," David says, then turns and heads out of the barn.

I find myself still looking around, admiring the chapel, as well as the sense of peace and calm that permeates the area around us.

"I like what you've done with this place," I note. "The whole place. It's ambitious and yet, simple."

"Well, some of us prefer to live a simpler life."

"I can see that," I reply. "I can see the appeal. Entirely self-sustaining?"

He nods. "We run on solar power and have a hydroelectric set up that runs from the river too," he says. "We've got a freshwater well, and a small aqueduct from the river."

"That's impressive."

Aaron smiles. "I'm assuming the heir to the Arrington media empire didn't come down here to talk about our set up," he says. "What can I do for you, Paxton?"

The fact that he recognizes me sends a shockwave

through me. I turn to him but don't recognize his face. I know I've never met this man before. Seeing my confusion, he laughs.

"I knew your father a bit. A long time ago. Another life, actually," he tells me. "I was an investment banker back then, but I gave it all up to run this place. Saw your dad socially every now and then. I even saw you around a few times."

I nod. "I'm sorry, I—"

"Oh, we never officially met. I just remember your dad singing your praises," he says. "It's not every trust-fund baby who gives up a cushy life as a media mogul to become a cop. It's an impressive story. I admire what you did."

"Thank you."

I guess in a way; my story mirrors his. He gave up a comfortable life for something simpler. And I have to say, he looks happy. Content. He looks like a man who's satisfied with his lot in life.

"There's always room for one more out here," he tells me.

"I'll give it some thought," I say and mean it.

"When you're ready, we'll be here."

"Thank you. I appreciate that," I reply. "As for why I'm here, I wondered if you recall Jacob and Karen Perry? I guess they used to be pastors here before you."

"Only by reputation. And let me tell you, it wasn't a good one," he tells me. "They were long gone when I bought the farm and refurbished it. The place had fallen into severe disrepair and needed a lot of work."

"Well, you did a pretty amazing job of bringing it back to life."

"Hard work is its own reward," he says. "But tell me, why are you asking about the Perrys?"

"Just doing some legwork for a case," I say. "I'm a PI now."

"Interesting work," he nods. "Also interesting that you're choosing to serve others."

"You can blame my wife for that."

"Oh, she could have only shown you the door that already existed in you," he says. "You're the one who needed to open it and walk through it."

"I suppose so," I nod. "Do you happen to know what happened to the Perrys? I can't find any records on them after they left this place."

"I wish I could tell you," he shrugs. "I never met them personally, only heard the stories. But it's like they up and disappeared one day. Some of their— congregants— took over and tried to keep the farm going for a while, but..."

He doesn't need to finish the statement. I know how it went. He swept in with a fistful of dollars, probably paid pennies on the dollar for the land, and built his perfect utopia. I don't begrudge him one bit for it though. Being a Captain of Industry is a cushy life, but it takes a toll on you eventually. Wears you down. Walking away from it with a fat bank account while you still have your health and sanity to live in an idyllic world like this is not a bad idea.

It's as I feared it might be though. Another dead end. I'd hoped to be able to track them down and give them my profile to see if it jogged their memory of somebody who might fit the description.

"Personally, I think those old hippies skipped on down to Mexico and are livin' free and easy on the beach down there," Aaron chuckles.

"That's a distinct possibility."

"Oh, but that reminds me," he says. "I have some boxes of stuff that belonged to them. After I bought the place, I had it all boxed up and stored. Just in case they ever came back. Been down there forever though. Maybe there's a clue to where they went in all that stuff."

That small spark of hope inside of me that was guttering and threatening to go out suddenly springs back to life.

"Excellent. Would you mind if I took a look?" I ask.

"Hell son, you can take the boxes for all I care," he shrugs. "If they haven't come back for them by now, they're not coming back. I'll have the boys load them up for you."

"Oh, that's not necessary," I say. "I can—"

He waves me off. "Like I said, hard work is its own reward," he says. "Besides, I caught the boys smoking behind the barn, so they need to work off their punishment anyway."

He flashes me a grin, and I follow him out of the barn. As the boys load the boxes into my Navigator, Aaron walks me around the compound a bit, telling me about it all. It's fascinating to me, honestly. He really has built his own little Eden out here on the outskirts of Kirkland. They're doing good works, helping a lot of people. It's admirable.

"How do you fund this place?" I ask. "If you don't mind my asking."

"Not at all. To be honest, between buying and renovating this place, installing all of the solar, and the aqueduct system, it ate through a big chunk of what I'd made in my career," he says. "I've still got a decent portfolio, but I'm hoping to save that for a rainy day. So mostly we rely on the tithing of the parishioners to keep our school and our drug programs going."

"Apparently, living simply is expensive," I remark.

Aaron laughs heartily. "Quite so," he says. "But still. I'd rather be broke living out here where I'm genuinely happy instead of having more money than God and being miserable."

"I admire you, Aaron," I say. "I have all the respect in the world for you."

"Kind of you to say so," he replies. "And I've got just as much respect for you, son. I admire what you did as well."

"I guess in our own ways, we were both called to serve."

"Exactly right," he smiles. "Well, I should get back

to it. Hope you find what you're looking for in those boxes."

"Thanks, me too. I appreciate you giving them to me."

He waves me off. "They were just taking up space in the cellar anyway."

He turns and starts to walk back to the chapel but stops and turns back to me.

"While I'm thinkin' about it, on the third Sunday of every month, we hold a barbecue and fellowship," he says. "I'd love it if you came by."

I nod. "I'd like that. Thank you."

He gives me a smile, then turns and heads for the barn again. I watch him go for a moment, secretly envying the look of absolute peace and happiness he had on his face. I wonder if I'll ever get a taste of that kind of life again. I had it once. For a little while anyway. But then Veronica died and it evaporated.

With a sigh, I walk out to my car. Maybe I'll have that life again someday. But for now, I have a mystery to solve and a good friend to save. And the clock is ticking.

TWENTY-SEVEN

Arrington Investigations; Downtown Seattle

"What is it we're looking for exactly?" Brody asks.

"Let you know when we find it."

"That's helpful."

I wish I could be more helpful, but I really have no idea what we're looking for either. I have all twelve boxes Aaron gave to me set up on the table in the conference room. We've slowly and methodically been working our way through them, examining everything closely, looking for something that will tip us off to Hayes and Blake's whereabouts— or about anything, really.

I glance at the clock and see that it's just past three. A little under nine hours to go. And with every tick of the clock, the deadline is looming larger. I have no doubt that if I don't find Hayes by midnight, that he will kill Blake. He is, after all, a man of his word. At least, he is when he chooses to be. And I won't gamble with Blake's life that this is one of those times.

"These boxes really stink."

"What do you expect? They've been in a cellar for almost twenty years," I point out. "It's not like he went down there and freshened them up every week."

"He's filthy rich. He should do that," Brody remarks. "I've seen rich people do stupider things with their money."

I laugh, knowing he's right. "Except that Aaron's not rich anymore," I tell him. "At least, not monetarily. He sank his fortune into the EFCC."

"I still can't believe he did that," Brody sighs, almost sadly. "That man was worth a mint. Like a literal mint."

"Hey, he's happy. You can see it in his face," I shrug. "He's the kind of satisfied and content we should all strive to be."

"I dunno man, that's a super weird vibe out there. You sure they weren't cannibals?"

"I promise they weren't cannibals."

"And you saw the kitchen? No bodies in the freezer?"

"I saw the farm."

"All I'm saying, man. Don't expect me to come riding to the rescue when it's your literal butt on the grill."

We both laugh. It's nice to have Brody here, even as stressful as this situation is.

"Honestly, the more I think about it, it does sound nice. But were there even any chicks out there?"

"Can't go wrong with a farmer's daughter."

Brody looks at me in wide-eyed surprise. "Wow. An hour at that place and you're loose enough to make sex jokes," he says. "I think you need to go live out there for a month. Who knows? Maybe you'll learn to laugh again. Or at least you'll make a nice dinner spread."

"Funny guy."

He shrugs. "I'm only half kidding."

"Yeah well, I'm only going to half kick your butt if you don't start digging through those boxes," I say. "We've got nine hours to save Blake's life."

The remainder of the running clock casts a pall over the conference room. We lapse into a grim silence and redouble back to work, examining the contents of the Perrys' life. Or at least, what's left of it. Maybe Aaron was right, and they cast aside all their worldly possessions to go frolic on the beach, living the life of a vagabond. Who knows?

Something inside me doesn't think so. There's just a nagging feeling growing inside of me, one that gets stronger with every box we open, that the Perrys never left that farm. Maybe having spent a decade seeing some of the worst of humanity, I've become jaded and cynical, automatically believing the worst in people. That's a possibility. But something is telling me the Perrys are in a shallow grave somewhere on the EFCC land.

Who put them there is another question entirely. I don't believe for a moment it was Aaron. I think in addition to making me cynical and jaded, ten years on the force also taught me to be a pretty keen judge of character. And I get nothing but a good feeling from Aaron. I truly believe he'd had enough of life at the top of the corporate food chain and just wanted something different. Something simpler. It's an impulse I understand and long for myself. So when he tells me he never met the Perrys, I believe him.

No, if they are still on that farm, buried somewhere on the land, I am certain it was at the hands of somebody they knew. Maybe one of the people who took over the EFCC after they 'left'. I'm certain it had to be somebody close to them. Somebody who stood to gain by their disappearance. But that is another case for another day.

Right now, the only concern I have, and the only case that matters, is finding out who Hayes really is and saving Blake. I toss the last of a bunch of useless papers into the box and slam the lid back down on it with a growl. I set the box down on the pile of boxes we've already gone through and grab the final one.

"If we don't find something here, we're screwed," I sigh. "I don't know what we're going to do. We're running out of time."

"We've got a little less than nine hours," Brody says. "We'll think of something."

I set my mind working on a Plan B as I take the lid off the final box. I dig out the first batch of papers, still not finding anything useful. Old magazine clippings, recipes, and other items. Nothing I can use. But then I pick up a manila envelope, open it up, and find a stack of old pictures. I feel a jolt of excitement in my heart even though I don't know if these are going to be any more useful than the recipe clippings.

Holding onto the photos, I drop the envelope and start to flip through them. These have got to be the Perrys. Candid shots of them in various places, doing various things. I recognize the farm in the background of some of them. There are a few of them in their preacher get-ups, standing at the pulpit, preaching away.

I can tell by their sweaty, flushed faces in the photos that they were definitely the charismatic, revival sorts of preachers. All sorts of gimmicks and stunts and choreography. At least on Sundays, since passionate preaching is what usually fills a collection plate. A couple of the other photos show them hanging out with their congregants. Sometimes even with joints in their hands.

When I get to one of the last photos in the stack, an audible gasp spills from my throat. I drop the rest of the photos and turn to Brody, showing him the picture.

"They had a son," I say.

"Nothing we found indicates they had a kid."

"And yet, there he is."

The photo shows Jacob and Karen standing with a young kid, maybe eleven or twelve, or so, in front of the Sequoia trees. The kid is wearing a Flock of Seagulls t-shirt and flashing a gap-toothed smile at the camera as Jacob and Karen stand behind him. Even though Brody is right and we found no other mention of a kid, this has got to be a family photo.

"So they have a kid," Brody says.

"This has got to be him. This has got to be Reuben Hayes," I say. "This has got to be the bastard who has Blake."

I go through my profile in my head and compare the timeline. Everything seems to fit. But we can't prove it. We already did a records search for Jacob and Karen, and there was no record of birth. This kid, if he is theirs, doesn't exist. At least not legally. No birth certificate, no social security number, no school records. Which means, if this is their kid, they had him at home. He wasn't born in a hospital. Which, given their secluded lifestyle, doesn't seem to be too far outside the realm of possibility.

"So how do we prove this is their kid? And how do we figure out who he is?" Brody asks.

"That's a good question," I say. "And we need to come up with a good answer pretty freaking fast."

I study the picture closely and look at the date stamp in the corner. August 1983. The last reported Perry sighting was in 1986. All mention of them in any of the old articles I read stops in November 1986. After that, all of the op-ed pieces, letters to the editor, or actual articles decrying the existence of this 'cult' in Kirkland, refer to somebody else named James Moore as the pastor.

"Okay, so they fell off the grid in November 1986," I say. "That would make the kid what, fourteen or fifteen, maybe?"

"Something like that."

"How many adoption agencies were there in Kirkland in 1986?"

Brody's fingers fly over the keys. He turns to me. "Just one," he says. "It was called Helping Hands. In fact, it's still called Helping Hands."

"Can you hack into their database?"

He arches an eyebrow and looks at me pointedly. "Please. It's not like I'm trying to hack into a federal criminal database. This is child's play."

I watch as he works the keys on his laptop like a maestro conducting an orchestra. I can see the excitement on his face as he does it. Yeah, Brody may protest and whine about doing these hacks for me, but he gets as big of a charge out of doing them as I do hunting killers. He stops and stares at his laptop for a moment and frowns.

"What is it? I ask.

He sighs and purses his lips. "Their digital files only go back to 1990," he says. "Anything before that hasn't been digitized yet."

"Figures," I growl and slam my fist down on the

table.

Silence descends over us for a moment. I weigh my agonizingly slim pile of options. I know I'm only working a theory here, but the more I think about it, the more I think I'm right. The kid in the photo, the unnamed child of Jacob and Karen Perry, has got to be Reuben Hayes. All of the different pieces of the puzzle fit. It has to be him. But without the file, I'm sunk.

"What do you think the chances are I can sweet talk some bitter receptionist into giving me the file?" I ask.

"Somewhere between slim and none."

"Yeah, that's what I thought.

I tap the edge of the picture against my chin as I think. There has got to be something I can do. Some way to get that file. And then the answer occurs to me. It's foolish and borderline insane, but it's the only plan I can come up with. So it's going to have to do.

"Where do they store those physical records? The ones from child's services in Kirkland," I ask.

Brody looks at me. "You cannot be serious."

"And yet I am. It might be the only chance Blake has," I say. "I want to know where Helping Hands keeps their physical records."

Brody whistles low and turns back to his computer, the keys clicking and clacking as he types away. Finally, he looks back up at me.

"There's an off-site warehouse near the shelter," he says. "They store everything there, apparently."

"Okay great. Text me the address," I say.

"You do know this theory of yours might not be correct."

"If you have a better competing theory, I'm all ears."

He falls silent and looks down at his laptop. I give him a grim nod.

"That's what I thought," I say.

I turn and hurry out of the office and out to my car. I need to get home to get dressed for my excursion. And though I'm loath to admit it with Blake's life on the line, there's a surge of excited adrenaline coursing through my veins. It's the same sort of rush I used to get when I was a cop and going on a raid. That surge of fear blended with nervous excitement that lights me up inside and makes me feel like I'm on fire.

I'm sure Blake, a law enforcement professional and veteran of her fair share of raids, would understand. But when I'm done with Hayes and I've gotten her out of there, I probably shouldn't mention it to her. Just in case.

TWENTY-EIGHT

Helping Hands Storage Facility; Kirkland, WA

Thankfully, the night is overcast and darker than pitch. It's like somebody up there is looking out for me. Who or whatever it is, I'll take it. I bypass the guard booth at the front of the facility and park on a street behind it, traversing through a public park to jump the fence that fronts a flood control channel. It's thankfully dry, so I run down one side and up the other, then walk to the tall fence topped with razor wire, hunkering down behind a bush.

I scan the rear grounds of the storage facility, looking for guards. Given how dark the night is, and the fact that I'm dressed like a ninja, I have no fear of being seen. Somebody would need excellent night vision to see me. And working in my favor, the guards I saw when I cruised by the front of the facility were carrying those ultra-bright cop flashlights, which will tip me off when they're coming my way.

"Okay, here goes nothing."

I set my backpack on the ground and take out the wire cutters. I then quickly cut a hole in the fence and push my way through it. Not seeing anybody on patrol, I dash across the open ground from the fence to the rear loading dock and make it without incident. I run up the ramp and am moving toward the back door, slipping my set of lockpicks out of my back pocket when I see it's been propped open with a standing ashtray. Clearly, somebody didn't want to be locked out when they stepped out to cop a smoke. That's a bit of good news for me.

I ease the door open and slip inside, carefully shutting it behind me. The light in the warehouse is dim, but it's enough for me to see by without having to risk turning on a flashlight. They aren't guarding this place like it's Fort Knox or anything, but I'm pretty sure they'd frown on me breaking into the place anyway. This section of the warehouse is filled with furniture and other essentials for the dormitories in the shelter.

I see a doorway on the far side of the building with a sign over the door marked 'records'. I make a beeline for it. Halfway there, I hear a door slam, the heavy echo of it reverberating around the warehouse. I freeze and duck behind a pallet full of mattresses wrapped in plastic. I strain my ears to listen and hear the footsteps of one of the guards. A moment later, I hear music and a man's deep, gruff voice singing along with Jay-Z.

My heart's hammering hard enough I'm sure he can hear me over his singing, I swallow hard and peer around the stack of mattresses. The man is tall and built like an NFL safety. Wide shoulders, lean build, and if he gets a running start, I'm sure he could blow me up like a missile hitting a wood bunker. I watch as he walks through the warehouse and disappears through a door that, when it closes, I see marked with the men's room symbol.

"Great," I mutter to myself.

Now I have to decide whether to wait where I am while he takes his evening constitutional or carry on with my business. I glance at my watch and see that it's eight o'clock. Time is starting to grow perilously short for Blake. That makes my decision for me, and I start to move.

I cross the rest of the warehouse at a run and slip into the records room, easing the door shut behind me. Pulling the penlight out of my pocket, I switch it on and sweep the room. It's a large room filled with row after row of shelving, and every shelf is stuffed with boxes. There are some empty shelves, and as I scan the tags, I take note that the boxes from the '90s are missing.

They're slowly but surely making their way to the digital age. But as it is with any and all underfunded bureaucracies, progress moves at a glacier's pace. I walk down the rows until I find the stack for 1986. I know what a longshot this is, but it's better than the no shot I had before. But if this fails, I'm not sure what I'm going to do.

"Think positive," I mutter.

I find the November 1986 box and pull it down. I sit down on the floor, so I'm partially shielded by boxes on the shelves. I'll be able to see anybody coming before they see me. Not that it will do me a lot of good since I'm surrounded by shelving, which means I'm trapped. But at least I'll have the element of surprise. It's not much but it's something, I suppose.

I take the lid off and set it aside then begin rifling through the files. There is a depressingly large amount of children who were taken into foster care in November 1986. And if I multiply this out by all twelve months, the number of kids put into the system, for one reason or another, is staggering.

"You're not here to solve the foster care system right now," I whisper to myself. "Do your job. Blake is counting on you."

Having mentally kicked my own ass, I dig into the box and immediately discard the files bearing girl's names. That leaves me with twenty-seven files. I flip them open one by one until I see a familiar face staring back at me. Gone, though, is the gap-toothed grin and, in its place, is a solemn, sober look. It's the look of a boy who knows he's been abandoned by his parents.

"Bingo," I say.

Though tempted to read the file now, I know I'm pressing my luck every moment I'm in here. I hear Blake's voice in my head and feel the smile tugging at the corners of my mouth despite the desperate and deadly circumstances.

"Patience you must have, my young Padawan."

She always says it to me as if I have a habit of going off half-cocked and running amok like a madman. That's a better description of her honestly, but I enjoy the irony when she says it.

I put all the rest of the files into the box and replace it on the shelf. I then take the file I came for and tuck it into my backpack, zip it up, and sling it over my shoulders again. After that, I creep to the door and quietly open it, peering out into the gloom of the warehouse beyond. I strain my ears but hear nothing. The silence carries a pressure all on its own, pressing down on me, making my body taut with tension.

I have no idea if Mr. Evening Constitutional is still in the bathroom or if he's gone already, so I need to be cautious. Opening the door, I slip out and immediately freeze when I see him in my peripheral vision.

"Crap," I mutter.

He's leaning against the wall casually, tapping his heavy flashlight against his palm like a billy club. My only saving grace right now is that he's not carrying a sidearm. I don't even see mace or a taser on his belt. All he's got is that flashlight.

"What's up?" he says with a smirk on his face.

"Came for the concert," I reply. "I heard you sound just like Jay-Z."

He chuckles. "So are we gonna have a problem here, ninja boy?" he asks. "Or are you gonna come to the security office with me all quiet and easy like?"

I smirk. "One thing you'll learn about me is I rarely do anything easy like."

"That's cool," he says. "I haven't beaten anybody in a dog's age. Been feelin' kinda rusty."

He stands up and starts making a show of limbering up, making sure I have a good view of his biceps. I cut my eyes to the door I came through, and all of a sudden, it seems like it's a mile away, rather than a hundred yards or so. The guard grins.

"I should warn you, I ran the 40 in 4.4," he says. "You won't make it to the door. I guarantee you that."

"Oh yeah? Why aren't you playing pro ball."

A sour look crosses his face. "Blew out my knee at the Senior Bowl."

"That's a tough break," I say.

He nods. "Sucks," he says. "Now, why don't you just take off the mask and come with me. It'll be easier for everybody."

"Thanks, but I'm going to have to pass. I have somebody really relying on me right now."

He shrugs his broad shoulders. "Okay man, have it your way," he says. "Just remember, I warned you."

"You did. And I appreciate it," I reply. "But how about you give me a three-second head start? Just to be sporting."

He laughs, his smile genuinely good-natured. "Yeah, all right. Just to be sporting," he agrees. "I'll count to three."

"Good enough. I appreciate your sportsmanship."

"You won't be sayin' that when I catch you and jam my foot up where the sun don't shine."

"Sure I will," I say. "But that's *if* you catch me."

He laughs out loud. "Go on, let's do this."

I don't even wait for him to say one when I take off like I was shot out of a cannon. I race across the warehouse and slip my hand into my pocket as I go. I hear him call three, and the chase is on. A sly grin curls my lips upward as I hear him closing in on me. The man was right. He's fast.

I hold off as long as I can, and just when I feel him closing the gap when I imagine him reaching for me, I whip my hand out of my pocket and scatter the handful of marbles I'd brought onto the ground behind me. I hear the little spheres of glass hit the floor and start to bounce, and a moment later, I hear the sound of him cursing up a blue streak as he slides on them.

I can't help myself and cut a glance behind me just in time to see his feet slip out from under him awkwardly, almost like he hyperextended his knee. A moment later, his legs come out from under him. And then, just like in a cartoon, his legs go up, and he lands on the concrete floor on his back with a loud grunt. He immediately grabs his knee and starts to writhe on the ground screaming in agony.

"Oh my God, it worked," I gasp.

A chuckle immediately bubbles out of my throat, but realizing his howling will bring the other guards, I turn and take off. I bang the door open as I go and don't even bother looking around me as I fly across the open ground, head down, arms and legs pumping. I make it to the fence without being caught, or anybody even shouting at me. I'm amazed. But as I stand at the hole I cut into the fence, I see the door bang open, and guards come spilling out of it like angry ants coming out of their hill to swarm the intruder.

"That's my cue," I mutter.

I duck through the hole and retrace my steps back through the park and to my car. I jump in and slam the door, then fire up the engine and quickly pull away from the curb. I check the rearview but don't see any of the guards in the street, finally letting out a long breath of relief.

"I made it," I gasp, feeling a surge of electricity flowing through my veins. "I can't believe I made it."

As I turn out of the residential streets and merge into traffic, I see a pair of cop cars, lights flaring, turn quickly onto the street I'd just exited. And as I drive away with my prize in my backpack, I'm struck by a feeling of relief that's so strong; I start to laugh. And once I do, I can't stop. At first anyway.

Once Blake's face flashes through my mind, I sober up real fast. I may have won one small skirmish, but the war is far from over. And the only battle that matters is still to come.

TWENTY-NINE

Arrington Investigations; Downtown Seattle

I slap the file on the table, and Brody looks at me with wide eyes and a look of stunned disbelief on his face.

"I cannot believe you got it," he says.

"Believe it."

"I thought for sure I was going to have to come bail you out of jail, man."

I shrug. "I've got a few tricks up my sleeve."

I tell him what happened at the warehouse, and that dumbfounded expression on his face only deepens. And when I'm done with my story, he gives me a crooked grin.

"Okay, one, I can't believe that marble stunt worked," he laughs. "What kind of cartoon bull is that?"

"Effective cartoon bull," I reply. "Where do you

think I got the idea?"

"Uh-huh. And two, that was pretty bush league, man," he grins. "Making him slip on marbles? Really?"

"Well, in my defense, he ran a 4.4 forty-yard dash," I say. "If I didn't cheat, I wouldn't be sitting here with the file right now."

"Fair point."

"Glad you agree," I say. "Now, can we figure this out?"

Brody nods, and together, we flip open the file and start to read. The first thing we both do is try to get to his name first. We both have a hand on the admissions sheet, reading the words, then turn to one another.

"Alvin Perry," we say in unison.

As Brody turns to his laptop, I start digging through the file, digesting all of the information I can. The more I know, the more I can weaponize that information and use it against him. Try to knock him off balance long enough to turn the advantage my way.

As I read his file, read about the neglect and abuse he suffered at the hands of his own parents, and then the few fosters he had, my heart actually goes out to him. It's no wonder Alvin Perry the adult has such a skewed, warped image of religion and relationships.

"This kid never had a chance," I sigh.

"Au contraire, mi amigo, he had a chance," Brody interjects. "He just chose to piss it away."

"Why are you mixing languages?" I ask.

"Because I'm barely literate in either."

"You're barely literate, period," I say.

He chuckles. "Anyway, this kid was smart."

"Still is smart."

"Fine. He's smart. But he won a full academic scholarship to U-Dub," he says. "Got a degree in English and Literature and became a teacher."

I sit back in my chair and look at him strangely. That was not what I expected. Like, not at all.

"A teacher?"

He nods. "Yup. Taught at Wagner High School in Kirkland, in fact."

"So he never left the area."

"Doesn't look like it," he tells me. "But get this, Alvin Perry goes dark after 1996. He just falls off the grid completely."

"And two years later, the murders begin."

Brody nods. "So he spent two years building a new identity and preparing himself for his mission."

"Exactly."

He probably spent those two years honing his craft, building his new identity, and building a war chest by ransoming kidnapped children back to their very wealthy parents. There likely won't be any records on that though. No police reports, no trail. But that doesn't matter anyway. It's window dressing.

The salient point here is that Alvin Perry essentially died in 1996, and someone new was born. He called it his becoming. His metamorphosis. Which means that his first kill, the most critical one and the one that shaped him, that launched him on this mission, took place in either 1995 or 1996. That would be my best guess.

"What are you thinking?" Brody asks.

"Look up murders in Washington state in the years 1995 and '96."

"That's casting a wide net."

"No choice."

Brody turns to his computer and starts typing away. He sits back, and as the data spools up, he looks over at me.

"We're looking at a little over five hundred," he says.

I tap my finger against my lips, thinking about how best to whittle this down.

"Okay, filter out all of the solved cases," I say. "We obviously know he was never caught. So unsolved murders only."

"Are you sure he even killed somebody in the state in those two years? What if he left for California? Most of the cases are there."

I shake my head. "I'm not certain of anything," I tell him. "But my gut is telling me we're on the right path."

As Brody does his thing, I glance at the clock and see that it's after ten. Time is running short. As if to emphasize the point, my phone buzzes with an incoming text message from Blake's phone. I call it up and look at it, feeling the knot in my gut tighten as I read the words.

Tick Tock, Paxton. Tick Tock…

"Okay, we're down to one hundred and seventy-five," Brody says. "Good call. It's better, but still a pretty hefty list."

I purse my lips and think harder. I work the profile over in my head and try to see how I can apply it to further narrow down the list. A moment later, the idea comes to me.

"Filter out every murder that involved a firearm," I tell him. "No guns at all. Also filter out cars, bow and arrow, and missile attacks if it's on there."

"Why is that?"

"Because Hayes— sorry, Perry— wouldn't dare use a gun. It's too impersonal for him," I explain. "He likes to be up close and personal with his victims. None of his known victims were shot. All of them were stabbed, bludgeoned, or strangled."

"Jesus," he says as he turns back to his laptop. "That's gruesome."

A moment later, he whistles low as he looks at the screen. Then he turns to me and turns the laptop so I can read the screen. I nod and feel a flash of triumph upon seeing that the list had been narrowed from one hundred and seventy-five to thirty-eight.

"People in rural Washington like their guns," Brody notes dryly. "More specifically, they like to kill other people with their guns."

It's good, but thirty-eight is still a lot of people. I can't think of another filter to apply to the search. With everything we've filtered out already, these thirty-eight are legitimate, and because he's an omnivore, there's no telling which is more likely, a man or a woman. But then another idea occurs to me. It might be a risk, but at this point, with the sand quickly running through the hourglass, it's one I'm willing to take.

"Filter out any murder vics who are prostitutes," I say. "Also, filter out the homeless."

"But aren't those his usual targets?" Brody asks. "That's his typical pattern."

I shake my head. "No. Not for his first kill. That one is special to him even still. It's the one he truly cherishes. His first vic is his ideal," I tell him. "And I'm certain it wasn't somebody living on the street or a prostitute."

"Okay, give me just a second here," he says as he applies another filter to the list. "That's really grim, man."

"Can you put it up on the big screen?"

Brody nods and is able to put his computer desktop up onto the conference room's large screen. I look at the list and nod approvingly as I see it's dwindled further, going from thirty-eight down to twelve.

"Welcome to the Emerald State, where we shoot a lot of people and murder bushels of prostitutes," Brody says. "I don't recall seeing that on the tourism pamphlets."

A wry smile curls the corners of my mouth upward. Twelve names. I look at them all, reading each one and commit it to memory as I do. Nothing stands out at first blush.

"Open up the first case file," I say.

Brody brings it up, and the second I see the photo of the dead seventy-six-year-old woman, I know she's not the one. He would never murder an elderly woman.

"Next file, please," I ask.

The next file comes up. It's an eight-year-old girl.

"Next."

I'm flying blind. I'm operating solely on instinct right now, and I'm suddenly scared that I'm playing Russian Roulette with Blake's life hanging in the balance. But I'm doing the best I can under the circumstances. I'm relying on my profile of the man, as well as my own intelligence, and the best-educated guesses I can manage to keep her alive.

The next file to come up is a thirty-five-year-old man. Drug user and a petty thief. He's a possibility, but he's not setting off the bells in my head.

"Save that one," I say. "And go to the next."

We go through the next five, with me saving two and discarding three. But when Brody brings up the next file, I freeze in my tracks. My eyes widen, and I feel a wild churning in my gut I can't deny. It feels like I have a river of ice flowing through my veins, and my heart picks up the pace.

"That's her," I say. "She's the one."

"How do you know that?"

"I just do," I say. "Let me see the particulars."

Brody calls up the case file, and I read it, taking in every detail. It was in October of 1996. Delia Johnson and her boyfriend Alex Ellison were asleep when they were attacked by a man wielding a knife. Alex was stabbed in the throat, and the killer left a vicious wound behind. He then took his time with Delia, drawing it out. Savoring it. In the end, he sliced her throat open and stabbed her body thirty-two times as she lay dying already. The coroner also indicates there was intercourse, but the state of a DNA lab in the nineties was unreliable, so there is no telling if she had intercourse that night with her boyfriend or was raped.

"This is it," I say. "This is the one."

"Are you sure? I mean, this is Blake's life on the line."

I nod. "Yeah. I'm sure," I tell him. "Great work, Brody."

He sits back in his seat, looking both relieved but also terrified. I know he's worried about Blake. So am I. But this is it. This is Alvin Perry's first kill. He looks over at me, his face etched with concern.

"So what now?" he asks.

"Now I set a date with a killer."

"Yeah, that sounds like a lot of fun."

"It will be," I tell him. "Tonight is the night we take out one of America's most prolific murderers."

I pick up my phone and compose my message:

Time to meet, Alvin.

Using his real name will get his attention. It'll show him that I'm serious and have the answer to his riddle. Now I just have to hope he truly is a man of his word.

THIRTY
ALVIN PERRY

Seattle Underground; Downtown Seattle

"Well look at this," I say, staring at the phone screen with a mixture of awe and admiration. "He is wonderful! He has learned my identity."

"Good. I'd hate for him to call you the wrong name when he shoots you in the face."

I laugh and shake my head. Special Agent Wilder is secured to the chair with a series of heavy, plastic zip cuffs. She's a physical specimen, but she's definitely not strong enough to reach behind her back and pull these apart. We're sitting in one of the hidden rooms of the Seattle Underground. And at this hour, it's completely deserted.

The walls around us are made of red brick and dried, cracked plaster. It's dim and carries the scent of dust, decay, mildew, and urine. It's not the most pleasant smell, but it is the perfectly symbolic place to play out the final act of our little melodrama. And also, since I know every inch of the Underground, it will make it easier for me to get away if this all goes sideways for some reason.

"Defiant to the end. That's all right," I tell her. "You enjoy yourself now because your time is almost up."

"So, you're a liar after all."

"How do you figure?"

"You told Pax that you'd let me go if he came up with the answer to your question."

"And I will. I will let you go," I tell her. "Whether you live or not is up to him. Not me."

"What in the world are you talking about?"

"Paxton has a decision to make coming up," I explain. "And it will determine the course of his life. And yours, I fear."

"He would never hurt me," she spits.

"Never?" I ask, arching an eyebrow at her. "Not even if it meant getting answers to questions that have plagued him since the night his wife died?"

Her eyes widen, and a look of shock crosses her face.

"You're full of crap," she gasps. "You don't have the answers to those questions."

"Don't I?"

"He'll see right through you," she snaps. "He'll know you're full of crap."

"I suppose we will see then, won't we?" I reply.

"And if you're right, you have absolutely nothing to worry about."

She shifts in her seat and struggles with her bonds. Not that it will do her any good. But I suppose it makes her feel better. More proactive and in control over her situation. She doesn't understand yet that she has no control over her situation. None. Right now, whether she lives or dies is in my hands. Soon, it will be in Paxton's. And if he chooses to forsake me, as part of me thinks he will, her life will once again be in my hands, because I will then kill them both.

"What happened to you?" she spits. "Forty lives. You murdered forty people. How do you sleep at night?"

"Very soundly, actually," I reply. "For I know I am doing the world a favor by cleansing it of the filth."

"From where I'm sitting, you're the only filth I can see."

"Yes well, your perspective is somewhat limited," I reply. "You are very intelligent and capable in your own way, do not get me wrong. But Paxton and I are simply on another level."

"You really do love yourself, don't you?"

I shrug. "Somebody had to."

"Awwwwww, did you not get enough love from mommy and daddy?" she fires back. "Are you punishing other people and taking their lives because you didn't get enough love at home?"

Her tone is mocking, and the sneer on her face is

vile. I grit my teeth and glare at her with every ounce of disdain I have for her. But she simply smiles in defiance.

"You are a walking cliché," she continues. "Do you even realize that? You wanna know how many losers exactly like you I've brought in over the years? Same old sob story? You're not special. You're not some untouchable god. You're nothing. You're just a sick freak who preys on people to feel better about yourself."

"And you are lucky I have not killed you yet," I hiss.

"You can't," she spits. "Because if you did, you would screw up your chance of pulling Pax into your twisted little fantasy world, and you know it."

She's good. Insightful and clever. And she's also horribly annoying. I glare at her for a long moment, summoning every ounce of strength and will I have.

"To answer your question, no I did not get loved at home. I was beaten, though. Often viciously. I was neglected and tormented. Abused," I tell her. "And the coup de grace was that when Mommy and Daddy decided they'd had enough of being parents, they simply dropped me at the nearest foster care facility and left."

She scoffs. "Cry me a river, you bastard."

A small, rueful smile touches my lips. "Unfortunately for them, they did not go far enough. When they found out the feds were looking into the church, they decided to change their names and run. They knew it would be harder with me in tow though, so they simply decided they'd had enough of being parents. Literally."

"Are you trying to evoke sympathy from me?" she asks. "Are you trying to make me feel bad for you?"

"No, I'm simply giving you the reasons I killed my parents."

The look of shock on her face is hilarious and makes me want to laugh out loud. She did not see that coming. Though, as a top-notch FBI agent, she really should have. All the signs were right there for her to see, after all. Wilder quickly composes herself, leveling her best icy glare at me.

"I'm not surprised," she says.

"You sure looked it."

She shrugs. "Nothing you do can surprise me anymore. I think you lost having that effect on me around victim number thirty."

"Ahhhh... victim number thirty was Andrew Fujita. Youth pastor. He would use his position to take advantage of teenage girls. I strung him up with rope from a cross in his own home. He was a fighter," I say. "But in the end, he gave in. Just as they all do."

It looks like she's physically suppressing a shudder. I disturb her. That's a fact I take some small measure of pride in. The fact that I can make an experienced and hardened FBI agent disturbed it quite the feather in my cap.

"Do you see why I do what I do? Who I target? Who I kill? I am not some uncouth madman merely lashing out in rage. It is all deliberate. Planned. Calculated. I cleanse this world of foulness and evil. I am a force for justice. Not unlike yourself, Agent Wilder."

I let out a chuckle that grows into a laugh, long and loud. It echoes against the empty brick walls, the sound twisting and folding back on itself, repeating and joining its own echoes as if to sound an entire chorus of laughter.

"Well, do you suppose it's time we call Paxton and get this show on the road?" I ask. "It's still early yet, but I suppose we don't have to wait until midnight. What do you think?"

"I think I'd like to see you die choking on your own blood."

"Always the charmer," I reply.

Standing before her, I find Pax's phone number and dial, then press the phone to my ear. He answers before the first ring has even ended.

"Alvin," he says, sounding chipper. "I suppose the jig is up."

"Oh no, we're not quite here yet," I say. "As I told you, there are decisions to be made and much left to discuss."

"Fine. Where are you?" he replies. "Let's discuss because I definitely have some things to say."

"Excellent. And am I correct in assuming you know the identity of my first kill?"

"I do."

"Very good. Then I suppose all that's left is the final stage of our game."

"Bring it."

I look over at Agent Wilder, and she's glaring balefully at me as she makes the symbolic gesture of struggling with her bonds.

"I asked you once how well you knew your wife. Do you remember?"

"Of course I do."

"And you feel confident that you knew her well?"

"Like I told you, she was my wife."

I switch the phone to my other ear, a Cheshire Cat grin spreading across my lips. "Wonderful. Then you should know where to go," I say. "Meet me in the place that scared her like nothing else."

"Scared her like—"

"Good luck. And remember, our appointment is for midnight. Do not be tardy. I don't want to be disappointed."

I disconnect the call.

THIRTY-ONE
PAXTON

Arrington Investigations; Downtown Seattle

"Scared her like nothing else?"
I stare at the phone for a long moment, wondering what he meant by that. Veronica was fearless. There was very little in this world that scared her. I turn to Brody. He knew her before I did. He was the one who introduced us all those years ago even.

"Do you know?" I ask. "Do you know what place scared her?"

He sits back in his chair and scrubs his face with his hands. He shakes his head and looks at me.

"I have no idea," he sighs. "She was never afraid of anything that I can remember."

I drop down into my seat and look at the clock. It's now past eleven, and the physical weight of the pressure I'm feeling is getting heavier by the second. I feel like

I'm about to be crushed beneath it. I listen to Perry's voice in my head again, replaying the conversation over and over again, trying to tease the meaning of his words out into the open. But nothing comes. I'm left staring at the top of the table, utterly clueless and feeling more helpless than I've ever felt in my life.

All I can do is sit there, staring at the clock, watching the second hand make its trip around the face, ticking off the minutes one by one. A sense of dread wells up within me as the realization that I may not be able to save Blake after all begins to settle down over my shoulders.

"This is garbage!" I roar, pounding the tabletop with my fist. "We got the answers. Against all odds, we got the answers he wanted, and he pulls this?"

"Slow down," Brody says. "Think."

"I am!"

This is the test. The real test. The one he wants me to fail because he knows it will push me over the edge. If I allow him to kill Blake, he knows I won't be able to stop my descent into darkness. It's what he's counting on because he believes it will force me to become just like him. He thinks that if I'm as powerless to save Blake, just as I was powerless to save Veronica, it will permanently break me, and I'll give in to my dark impulses.

But what he doesn't realize is that this pursuit of him has changed me. It has made me see myself in a completely different way. This investigation has revealed pieces of me I never knew existed before. It's helped me see myself the way Veronica did. And while it might be hard for me to accept at first, holding fast to those things, to what Veronica tried so hard to help me see, is what will keep me alive and functioning. Only that will keep her alive inside of me.

Those things cannot be broken no matter what he does to me. Those realizations and revelations I've had as we've chased him have taken root deep inside of me. They're already buried deep underground—

"That's it," I gasp, sitting up straight, my eyes wide, and my heart pounding with excitement.

Brody looks over at me. "What's it?" he asks. "What did you figure out?"

"Do me a favor, call up Veronica's article from October sixteenth, 2017."

It was one of the last pieces she wrote before she died. I keep her website up and functional, as well as her archive of podcasts. She was just getting started really, but she'd developed a loyal following that was growing by the day. Keeping her website running is my way of keeping her alive for them as well. And every now and then, one of her fans will stop by the website and leave a message for her. In a way, seeing how much others loved her helps me too.

I get to my feet and look at the big board as Brody calls it up. The article is titled *Seattle Underground, Separating Fact From Fiction.* Because it was October, Veronica thought it would be fun to do a Halloween piece, and because the Underground is reportedly haunted, she arranged to take a private tour one night. I remember her coming home pale as a ghost herself. We drank wine and laughed about it all night.

I read the text of the article. It's not long before I find what it is I'm looking for. It's a line in the article near the end.

"...I don't consider myself easily spooked, and I can't confirm the validity of the alleged ghost sightings, but there is something about the Seattle Underground. There's a certain mystique to the way the shadows flit between the cracks in the walls. The dead ends and closed-off pathways. The glimpses of the still-standing past. The secrets hidden by years and years of neglect. Whatever truly lurks at the heart of the Underground will have to remain a mystery. For now, it's a place that seems to reveal more questions for every answer you uncover. And that place scares me like nothing else."

Brody looks over at me. "Do you really think it's the Underground?"

I nod. "I do," I say. "I'm sure of it."

"Okay, let's go," he says.

I shake my head. "No, you're not going anywhere near the guy," I say. "I'm not going to be responsible for anybody else getting hurt."

"You do know him taking Blake was not your fault."

"He never would have known she existed if not for me."

"He bugged the office, man."

"Still. I don't want to risk your life too," I tell him. "Please. Just stay here and be ready if I do need you."

He opens his mouth to argue but closes it again and nods. "You got it, man. Whatever you need. I'll be ready."

I clap him on the shoulder and give it a squeeze. "You're my best friend, Brody. You've always been there for me—"

"Shut up. Don't you even dare start talking like you're not coming out of this," he snaps. "Go do what you do best— beat the crap out of him, grab Blake, and get back here. That's what you do. That's what you're going to do. You got me?"

"I got you."

I squeeze his shoulder again and pull him into a tight embrace before heading out of the office. I didn't say it because I didn't want to freak him out any more than he already was, but I have a bad feeling as I head into what might be my final confrontation with Alvin Perry. Never before in my life have I ever felt this outmatched. He always seems to be two steps ahead of me, and even though I've closed that gap a little bit, the gap still exists.

He's managed to get under my skin and rattle me in ways nobody ever has before. Not even my father. And I know he's going to have some nasty surprises waiting for me when I get there. This is not going to be a bloodless coup. We are both fighting for something, and we are both the type who will fight to the death for it. It's very possible that I may not come out of this alive.

But I will make sure to do everything in my power to make sure that Blake does. She's the mission, and she is my focus. Everything else, including my own life, is extraneous and disposable.

THIRTY-TWO

Seattle Underground; Downtown Seattle

The Underground is closed for the day, but I see the gates that lead to the entrance have already been pried open. The door is popped and standing slightly open, beckoning me. I pull my weapon out of the holster on my hip and check the magazine, then slam it home before I chamber a round and turn the safety off. My concealed carry permit hasn't come just yet, but it's close enough.

I pull my coat around me tighter, concealing the holster as best as I can. I open the door and pull out the small penlight I have and sweep the area in front of me. Nothing. It's clear. The lights inside are dim, leaving most of the area around me in shadows and gloom as I descend the staircase.

After the Great Fire back in 1889 leveled a lot of the city, Seattle was rebuilt right on top of the remains of the old city. But the rebuilding left a labyrinth of passageways, basements, and other assorted rooms. It's a ghost town, a relic of the past, living just below the streets of one of America's biggest cities.

Eventually, some enterprising mind figured out how to make a few bucks off the old ghost town, and since then, the Underground has become one of Seattle's bigger tourist attractions. It is literally like stepping into the past. Relics and artifacts of the bygone era remain, as does all of the original construction. Oh, they've had to make improvements here and there to ensure the place doesn't collapse and kill the tourists— that would be bad for business after all— but it's relatively unobtrusive and doesn't detract from the flavor of the old city.

Personally, I like it down here. I know a lot of people don't. Some feel creeped out, and others are certain they see ghosts. Paranormal garbage notwithstanding, it's the fact that it harkens back to a simpler time that draws me. And if you listen closely, you can hear the echoes of the past. I've always found a pleasant charm about the Underground.

But not tonight. Tonight there is nothing charming or simple about it. Tonight the Underground may become a tomb. I just know that it won't be a tomb for Blake. I'm going to get her out of here if it kills me.

Up ahead of me, I see a faint green glow on the

ground, so I walk to it. I squat down and pick up the green glow stick. I look up the corridor and see another. This is obviously the path Perry wants me to follow. And so I do. I follow the trail of green glow sticks and quickly realize we're veering off the normal path laid out for the tourists. I'm entering areas that are restricted from customers, as they've been deemed too dangerous.

The winding path takes me about ten minutes to navigate, and when I step through a large hole in a brick wall, I see Blake tied to a chair at the other end of the room. She looks up at me with wide eyes, but the gag in her mouth prevents her from communicating with me. I scan the room but don't see Perry anywhere. Blake is shaking her head vigorously though, tears glimmering in her eyes and spilling down her already wet cheeks.

The sight of Blake in tears stops me in my tracks. A wave of trepidation flows through me. She is not the crying type. I've never seen her cry before. And I know she is crying for me. Because I may not come out of this alive.

"Welcome, Paxton," comes Perry's voice. "And thank you for arriving on time."

"I'm a man of my word," I throw his words back at him. "Now, let Blake go."

"All in due time."

The walls of this room have plenty of holes and are collapsed in some places. I narrow my eyes, trying to see through the darkness that hangs thick and deep in the cavernous emptiness. He could be standing anywhere beyond that veil of pitch, and I wouldn't be able to see him. And the acoustics in here distort his voice, making it seem like it's echoing in from everywhere, adding to the confusion. I can't pinpoint his location by his voice because of it. That's probably why he picked this room.

"You got me here, Perry," I call into the darkness. "Now cut her loose. That was the deal."

"This is true. And I will not renege on it, I assure you," he replies. "But I wanted to make you an offer before we do that."

"You have nothing I want."

"Do not be so sure about that, Paxton."

Blake keeps shaking her head vigorously. She's trying to warn me off about something, I can tell, but until I can get that gag off her, she can't tell me what. It makes me uneasy, but it's also making me more vigilant than I already am. Keeping my back pressed to the wall, I start to circle the room, edging toward the other side where Blake is. I keep my eyes moving, taking in the room around me as best as I can.

"Tell me something, Alvin, did you murder your parents before or after you murdered Delia Johnson and Alex Ellison?"

His laughter and slow applause ring out, coming at me from every direction, but I keep going, half worried that I'll catch a knife in the back from one of the holes in the wall before I get to Blake.

"Congratulations on putting together the mystery of

my life," he says, punctuating it with loud claps. "It sounds like you have me all figured out."

"Not completely. It's like I told you, we all need our secrets," I tell him. "But I have a pretty good idea of who you are and why you do the things you do."

"Bravo, Paxton. Bravo," he says. "As far as my parents go, it was Delia who allowed me to kill them. It was her sacrifice, her contribution to my becoming, that gave me the skills and confidence to hunt them down and begin my work."

"Yeah, that's not twisted or anything."

"Do not be so quick to judge," he scolds me. "Not all of us grew up with the privilege you did."

That is very true. I acknowledge that. But the brittleness of his voice when he said it tells me that I was right about him. He's jealous of how I grew up. I am more of a symbol to him, a reminder of the life he wanted so badly. This game was never about me. It was all about him.

"You did not have parents who harangued and beat you daily," he goes on. "You did not have parents who deprived you of the basics."

"That's true," I acknowledge, still trying to keep him talking and find his location. "But it's not like I grew up in Nirvana either. Even people with money have problems, Alvin."

"Do not compare your upbringing with mine," he snaps. "They are nothing alike."

"You might be surprised, actually."

I make it to Blake and squat down to assess the cuffs. Plastic zipcuffs. But just as I'm about to reach for my knife to cut them off her, I notice the box underneath the chair. It's square, made of metal, and has a timer on it. The red glowing numbers show ten seconds.

"Jesus Christ," I mutter.

I pull Blake's gag down and stare into her eyes. She looks back at me, her face drawn and pale, her green eyes alight with both fear and rage.

"Stay very still," I tell her. "There's a bomb under your seat."

She gives me an exasperated look. "Yeah, duh. I know," she snaps. "That's what I've been trying to tell you."

"Oh. Well..."

I get to my feet and turn in a circle, turning my attention back to deciphering where Perry is. But he remains invisible to me.

"A bomb, Perry? Really?" I hiss. "You said you were a man of your word."

"I am," he replies. "I'm not going to do anything to her. You will decide whether she lives or dies."

"Fine. She lives."

"Not so fast, Paxton."

A low growl escapes my throat, and I narrow my eyes. "What?" I snap.

"The deal I was set to offer you before. It's time," he says.

"What deal?" I ask, barely able to keep the hostility

out of my voice to comply with Perry's 'pleasant demeanor' and politeness rule.

"It's simple, really. I know you're not satisfied with the conclusions drawn in your wife's death," he says. "You don't believe the conclusions."

"Wow, genius-level detective work, Perry. Good job."

"Watch your attitude, please," he replies. "What if I told you I had information about that night? About her accident that might put things in an entirely different context for you? What if I showed you that you are correct to question everything?"

"I'd say you are full of crap," I fire back. "I've been digging into this for two years. You've been on it for two days. I think I've covered everything and highly doubt you uncovered something I didn't."

He laughs softly. "Are you willing to take that chance? Are you willing to let me walk away, not knowing whether or not I have some information that might blow your wife's case wide open?"

"I don't believe you," I tell him.

"I can see that," Perry replies. "But on my word, on my honor, I vow to you that the information I am holding puts the entire accident, if it was that, in an entirely new light."

"You know he's trying to get into your head, right?" Blake whispers to me.

I nod my head, but deep down, I wonder. He puts a

lot of stock in his word. In his honor. I don't think he'd offer those up if he wasn't being sincere.

"And what do I have to do to get that information from you?" I ask, trying to sound completely bored and unconvinced.

"You will come with me. You will let me guide you onto the path that will allow you to build upon my legacy," he says. "And also, you will pull the trigger that will set off the bomb underneath Special Agent Wilder."

I open my mouth to reply but hesitate. All of a sudden, I can't seem to form the words. The idea that I could finally put Veronica— and my mind— to rest once and for all, is appealing. It's something I've desired for so long. All those sleepless nights. All those lingering questions that have haunted me for the last two years. They could all be put to rest. I would have the answers I need to move on with my life.

And here's Perry, dangling that in front of me.

"Pax, you know he's full of crap, don't you?" Blake hisses, a note of worry in her voice. "He's trying to play you."

I give her a small smile, but it does nothing to reassure her. Instead, her face becomes even more pale, and she looks at me like I've already pulled the trigger on the detonator.

"On your honor, you say you have information about Veronica's death? Where did you get it?" I call out.

"That doesn't matter and is not your concern," Perry

replies. "All that matters is that I have it and am willing to give it to you."

I look down at Blake again, giving her a look of pure sadness, and try to convey my silent apology to her. Her eyes widen, and her lips tremble. She stares at me in stunned shock, unable to conceive of a world where I'd do this to her.

"Pax," she stammers. "Pax, don't do this. Please."

"You know how bad I want those answers, Blake. How long I've been searching for them?"

"You're going to kill me, Pax," she cries. Fresh tears roll down her cheeks. "You're going to murder me. You'll be just like him."

"But I'll have the answers I've been driving myself crazy over for the last two years."

"Paxton Arrington—"

I lean down and kiss the crown of her head, cutting off her words. Instead, she breaks down into a series of wild, loud sobs.

"I'm sorry, Blake. Please forgive me."

I wrench my eyes shut and turn away from her.

"I want the information, Perry."

He steps out of the shadows, a wide smile on his face. I was right. He is nondescript, of sorts. But I recognize him clear as day. He was the IT guy Brody hired. He was the cable guy at the Morgans'.

And he's the man who's ruined my life.

He laughs, and for all the world, looks at me the way a proud father looks at his son.

"I knew you would," he says. "I even told her you'd choose Veronica over her."

"I already did once before," I reply, drawing a wide-eyed stare from her.

"That's where the chemistry I sense between you two comes from," he responds. "An unrequited love. Sad."

"Give me the information about Veronica," I demand.

"In due time. Right now, you need to prove yourself to me, Paxton," he says. "I need to see that you are committed to ascending. To transforming."

"I'm committed enough," I snap. "Just tell me what you want me to do."

He pulls a triggering device out of his pocket and hands it over to me. I reach for it, only to have him yank it away at the last minute. Perry gives me a beatific smile.

"She will be your Delia Johnson, Paxton," he says. "She will be the one who sets you free with her sacrifice. And she will help you start your metamorphosis. Don't forget to thank her for her contribution to your becoming."

I nod and take the trigger out of his hands and turn to Blake. I give her a small smile. Her cheeks are wet with tears, and her eyes are red and puffy. She sniffs loudly, and I see her entire body trembling.

"Thank you," I say.

"What are you thanking her for, Paxton?" he asks me from behind.

"Thank you, Blake Wilder, for showing me who I truly am."

I whip my head around now to a confused and shocked expression on Perry's face. But he recognizes the threat instantly and starts to react. I see the snarl cross his face, but his motions are too slow. I round on him and drive my fist flush into his nose with a sound like hitting the old leather of a mitt. Perry's head snaps backward. He staggers back a couple of steps, and blood flows from his nose, running down his neck and painting his light blue shirt with streaks of crimson.

I press my advantage and rush him, but Perry is ready for me. He swings the blade I never saw him palming. I barely jump backward in time to avoid being totally disemboweled. As it is, I've got a long, shallow cut crossing my torso, and I already feel warm, tacky blood flowing down my stomach.

Before he can get his blade back around though, I grab him by the wrist and start to bend it backward. He lets out a squeal of pain, and so I drive my other fist into his face again. This time, I hear his nose snap. The blood flows freely, giving him a gruesome visage.

Somehow, he manages to buck me off of him and spin away. Perry lunges at me, blade first, and as I dodge it, I realize too late that it was a feint. And before I can react, I feel his blade sink deep into my arm. The pain is excruciating. I let out a howl of agony.

I quickly stagger back, taking Perry's blade with me. He reaches for it, but I'm quicker this time, and lash out with my foot, sweeping his legs out from under him.

Perry hits the ground with a loud grunt but starts to get up again right away, so I step forward and drive my foot square into his jaw. I hear something inside snap, and Perry falls forward, falling face-first onto the combination wood and stone floor. He doesn't move for a moment. I fear I might have killed him.

The irony isn't lost on me. I fear I might have killed this absolute monster, who has not hesitated to kill dozens. But the selfish part of me is still holding onto the possibility of his answers. I regret that I could have killed the one man who could have told stories, named names, and given me the information I've sought for so long. It leaves a hollow feeling in the center of me.

But then he stirs. I'm hit with an overwhelming wave of relief and let out a long, shaky breath. He's alive, just out cold. I turn back to Blake and give her a smile. I move behind her and cut her zipcuffs off. She quickly gets to her feet and takes a moment to work the stiffness out of her muscles. Then she steps forward and delivers a vicious kick to the unconscious man's midsection.

"Bastard," she spits on him. And then she turns and slaps me hard across the face. "And that's for making me think you were actually going to do it."

"Oh ye of little faith," I chuckle, nursing my cheek with my good arm.

"Or maybe you're just that good of an actor. And a bastard."

"Probably a bit of both."

I see Blake looking at me and see the adrenaline that's been pumping her up the last couple of days ebbing and know she's about to collapse. I pull Blake to me and hold her in a tight embrace. She melts against me, her entire body going limp. Eventually, she's able to stand on her own again. She uses the sleeve of her shirt to wipe the tears from her face, and she sniffs loudly.

"We need to call the cops," she says. "Mr. Perry here is going to be going away for a very long time."

"You should probably call the bomb squad too," I say. "Just in case."

"That's a good idea. And an ambulance," she nods, pointing at the knife still lodged in my arm.

I look at the fallen man. He's still out and hopefully having pleasant dreams because where he's going, it's nothing but a waking nightmare day after day after day. We find some rope and quickly tie his hands and feet, using double and triple knots. When he comes to, we don't want to have to battle him again, and then we sit down on the far side of the room as Blake calls the cops, fills them in on what's happening, and requests assistance.

"Come on," I say. "Let's get out of here and go get some fresh air. He's not going anywhere."

"That's a fantastic idea."

Leaning heavily against each other, knife still

protruding from my arm, we walk out of the Underground and into the cool, night air. As we walk, she looks up at me, a curious expression on her face.

"Were you the least bit tempted to trade me for that information?" she asks.

"I'd be tempted to trade you for a Snickers bar," I scoff. We both share a laugh, echoing up into the evening air.

THIRTY-THREE

Arrington Investigations; Downtown Seattle

It's been two weeks since our showdown in the Underground, as one local paper called it, and the phones have not stopped ringing. More work than we can handle and more interview requests than that. I guess that tends to happen when you help take out one of America's most notorious serial killers.

It's been so crazy here lately, we had to hire a receptionist to field the calls for us. And I'm already thinking about bringing on another investigator or two to help handle the overflow cases. Which is what I'm doing right now: poring through resumes. It's not a very easy task when you've got one arm in a sling.

"How's the arm?"

I look up from my coffee and see Blake standing in my office doorway.

"Hurts still," I tell her.

"Don't be such a baby. It was a flesh wound,"

"Tell that to the muscle they had to surgically repair."

She's got a warm smile on her face, but I can tell that something is going on. Something's bothering her.

"What is it?" I ask. "What's wrong?"

She leans back in her chair and crosses her legs, pursing her lips and looks away from me. Whatever it is, it's tough for her to take. I can tell.

"Were your bosses not impressed with how great you are?" I ask. "I mean, you took out a man who's murdered over fifty people."

"That's the thing... they are impressed," she says. "I'm getting promoted."

"Hey, that's fantastic. Congratulations."

"Thanks." Her voice is tinged with sadness. "But the promotion is in New York."

I lean back in my chair and whistle low. "That's a long commute."

She laughs. "At least it's not congested too badly. I can probably make decent time."

"Yeah, two or three days, tops."

She laughs and shakes her head. "Thanks. I needed a laugh."

"Anytime. Listen, I know it sucks, but it's a promotion," I tell her. "You have to take it because I guarantee if you don't, there may not be another one coming for a long time. People remember being turned down and not too fondly."

"Yeah, I know," she replies. "I was just hoping you'd tell me not to go."

"Well, when you fall flat on your face in your new job, you know where to find me," I say. "And we are always looking for trained investigators. We'll even take Bureau scraps."

She laughs wildly. "You are such a jerk."

"I've been told it's one of my best qualities."

"You've been lied to."

We both fall silent for a moment, each of us contemplating her impending move. She is often out of town, and we sometimes go several months without seeing each other. But she always came home to Seattle. Always. And this time will be different. This time, she's not coming home. I hate the idea of losing my friend—one of my only friends, truth be told.

"When do you go?" I ask.

"End of the week."

I purse my lips and nod. "It's going to suck with you gone. Especially with only Brody here," I grin. "But I'm proud of you. You deserve this, Blake. And besides, you have got to milk this whole, 'I bagged a serial killer' thing for all its worth. Take advantage of it while it lasts."

She laughs and nods. "I do," she responds. "But this will be a good time for you to get out and meet new people. Socialize."

"Yeah, I don't think so." I pause, looking at her for a long moment. "I am going to miss you though."

"And I'm going to miss you too."

My cell phone rings, interrupting the moment. Blake looks away, and I see her cheeks flush as I pick up my phone and connect the call.

"Arrington."

"Mr. Arrington," comes the familiar voice. "Lovely to hear your voice again."

"Wish I could say it was mutual. What do you want, Perry?"

Blake looks at me; her interest piqued when she hears who's on the other end of the line.

"I'd like to talk to you," he says.

"So hurry up and talk. Isn't phone time expensive down there in prison?"

"No, no. Face to face," he replies.

"Not happening. You have a great day—"

"I reconsidered, Paxton," he cuts me off. "I'll give you the information I found on your wife."

I'm taken aback by his words and stare at Blake. "Really? Why the change of heart?"

"Because we only have so long on this planet," he tells me. "And I'd like to leave this world with a clean conscience."

I purse my lips and nod. "Okay, so can you just go ahead and tell me?"

"I can't. It has to be face to face."

"But why?" I ask.

"Because those are my rules."

I pinch the bridge of my nose and growl under my breath. Perry is doing his best to assert control of the situation. Control over me. What else is new? But if it gets me the information I want— have wanted for years — it could be well worth it.

"Okay," I finally relent. "Face to face."

"Excellent," he beams. "I'll look forward to your visit then."

I disconnect the call and drop my phone on my desk. Blake looks at me for a long moment in silence.

"Guess I'm going to jail," I mutter.

EPILOGUE

King County Correctional Facility; Seattle, WA

The harsh buzz echoes in my ear as the gate slides open in front of me. I walk through and am frisked by one of the correction officers while a second runs the metal detecting wand over me.

"Your buddies did this two gates back," I say. "Do you really think I stuffed an automatic rifle under my clothes between there and here?"

"Protocol," the guard who'd frisked me says.

"The first group of guys could have missed a grenade up your sphincter when they wanded you the first time," the other guard gives me a smirk.

I chuckle. "Fair enough."

"He's good to go," shouts the first guard. "Open three."

The harsh metallic buzz sounds again, and another gate opens in front of me. I'm ushered through the gate, then down a long hallway. I pass through another door and find myself in a room with a row of booths before me. Each booth has a chair and a telephone receiver on the wall and is separated from the other side by a thick sheet of plexiglass.

Of the eight booths, three are occupied. I pick the one that's furthest away from everybody and sit down to wait. It's against my better judgement to be here, but Reuben Hayes— or rather, Alvin Perry— promised me information that I would want about Veronica that specifically related to her death. Thinking of him as Alvin Perry and not Reuben Hayes is still taking some getting used to, despite the fact that I always knew Hayes was an alias. His real name doesn't feel quite right in my mouth just yet, though.

He wouldn't give it to me over the phone, saying he'd only give it to me in person. One last face to face. No doubt to try and convince me one final time to pick up his mantle and build on his legacy. Given that there are officially fifty-two bodies to his credit, I'm relatively certain Alvin Perry's legacy is pretty secure on its own without any help from me.

I check my watch and stand up, trying to see the door to the prison on the other side of the glass. There's a CO on the door, but nobody coming through. I grunt and sit back down, irritated that he's making me wait.

Given that this is the final time I'll see him, and he knows it, Alvin is trying to pull the ultimate power play by making me wait. One last grasp at retaining control over me.

I would say screw it and leave if I didn't desperately want the information he's got. Or at least, that he claims he's got. Part of me doesn't want to believe him. Wants to think this is just some attempt at control. One last game.

But the rest of me isn't willing to take that chance. If he has some bombshell about Veronica's investigation, I want it. Need it. And if it ends up being a dry hole, merely a case of him just screwing with me again, all I've lost is a few hours of my day. I'll willingly make that trade any day of the week.

"Arrington?"

I turn around and see the guard from earlier leaning in the doorway— minus his wand. I give him a curious expression.

"Yeah?"

"Can you come with me please?"

I point to the glass. "I was waiting—"

"I know. It's about that," he replies. "Come with me, please."

Feeling uneasy, I get to my feet and cross the room, walking out the door. The guard leads me quickly through a series of corridors, looking around nervously the whole time. Something feels really off to me. I'm just giving thought to turning back when he ushers me into an empty office, which immediately sets the warning bells off in my head.

I turn around to push my way past him and back to the visitation room, but he closes the door and blocks the way. He's a big guy who obviously works out a lot, but I'm pretty sure I can take him. Or at least get in a few good shots before he takes me out.

"What is this about?" I demand. "Get away from the door and let me out of here right now."

He holds his hands up in surrender to show me he's not a threat. "I'm sorry I ambushed you like this. I just don't know who to trust right now, and I have a message for you."

My uneasiness ebbs slightly, but my curiosity spikes. "What's going on? What are you talking about?"

"It's Mr. Perry. Alvin Perry," he says. "The guy you were here to see."

"Yeah, I'm aware of who he is."

He runs a hand through his crew cut, his face flushed, and beads of sweat standing out on his forehead. The man is nervous. More than nervous, really. I'd say the man is downright terrified. I look for his name badge but see that he's taken it off, deepening my sense of unease again. I don't know what's happening, but I'm getting the sense that whatever it is, it's bad. Very bad.

"What's your name?" I ask.

He opens his mouth to reply and then shakes his head. "I'd prefer you not know. No offense and nothin' against you, but with the way things are right now, I don't want my name anywhere near this."

"Okay. I understand," I nod. "No names. Now, what's going on?"

He blows out a breath and mops the sweat off his brow. "It's Mr. Perry. He's... he's dead."

My eyes grow wide, and my heart drops into my stomach. That was about the last thing I expected him to say. I feel like a mule just kicked me in the gut. I mean, I should be celebrating. One of the most prolific serial killers in the history of our country is dead. That's not a bad thing.

But he had information I wanted. Information I needed. And with him dead, I'm not going to get it. Those questions will continue to linger in my head. Perhaps even worse, now that I know how close I came to possibly being able to answer them. But they're gone. Like a puff of smoke on the breeze, they're just gone.

"H-how?" I ask. "How did he die?"

"Hung himself in his cell."

I look at him in disbelief. I'd expected that maybe he'd been shanked by a bigger, meaner inmate. Maybe beaten to death. Maybe he had a heart attack. The last thing I expected was to hear that he took his own life.

But once the initial wave of shock wears off, I look at the man as my disbelief sets in. Alvin Perry was a malignant narcissist. People like him are so self-absorbed, they would never kill themselves. It's not an absolute, of course, but nine times out of ten, a malignant narcissist would never kill themselves.

"I don't believe that," I tell him. "Not for a second."

"Yeah, me either," he replies. "But that's the official story around here. Somebody on the night shift found him hanging from his bunk with his bedsheet wrapped around his neck."

"That's crap," I say, shaking my head.

"I can't really speak to that. You're goin' to have to check out the autopsy on your own," he says. "I'm only talkin' to you because I made a promise to Mr. Perry."

"Okay, promised him what?"

I watch as the man slips an envelope out of his pocket and walks it over to me. I take it from his trembling hand and look up at him.

"What has you so spooked?" I ask.

He looks back at the door like he's expecting somebody to come bursting through it to haul him away.

"Mr. Perry told me it was goin' to happen," he practically whispers. "Told me they were goin' to kill him. Said they'd kill everybody who knows what he knows."

"Who?" I ask. "Who's going to kill him?"

He shakes his head. "Don't know and don't want to know," he replies. "I've got a wife and kids, and I don't want to know."

I start to tear open the envelope, and he lets out a choked gasp. I stop tearing and look at him.

"What?" I ask.

"Whatever is in that envelope is radioactive, man,"

he replies. "Mr. Perry died for it. I'd prefer it if you waited until you were out of here before you opened it. Like I told you, I've got a wife and kids."

I nod and slip the envelope back into my pocket. "Fair enough."

"Okay, time's up. I need to get you out of here."

I follow the guard back out to the main reception area. As we make our way through the jail, I can't help but feel like I'm being watched. I feel eyes on me at every turn, and every time I pass a guard, I feel like they're scrutinizing me a little too closely. The man leading me is no less nervous, jumping at every sound, and acting like he expects to be murdered where he stands.

By the time we make it to the main gates, I felt as emotionally spent as he looks. I turn and am about to speak, but he beats me to the punch.

"I don't know you. You don't know me. And I didn't say or pass nothin' to you," he says.

"My sentiments exactly."

He closes the gate in my face and turns, scurrying off quickly. I do the same and head back to my car, strange thoughts and conspiracy theories running through my head. By the time I get behind the wheel of my Navigator again, I'm positive that Perry didn't kill himself. It just doesn't fit with my profile of him. It doesn't fit with the profile of malignant narcissists in general. As a rule of thumb, they just don't kill themselves.

With hands trembling from both anticipation and trepidation, I tear open the envelope and slide out the single sheet of paper. I drop the envelope in my lap and unfold the page, carefully reading the neat and precise penmanship of the late Alvin Perry, and feel a chill slither down my spine, sending an army of goosebumps marching across my skin.

I've never been a particularly superstitious or spiritual man, but it feels like he's reaching out from the grave to speak to me. It's just creepy. I read the message several times over, trying to grasp what it is he's saying but come up completely empty. Except for his last-ditch effort to recruit me to his murderous cause.

Paxton,
The game is still afoot. If you want to know why your wife died, look into something called Xytophyl.
All the best,
Alvin Perry, aka Reuben Hayes
PS: It is never too late to become what you were meant to be.

I stare at the page, not comprehending anything at the moment. Xytophyl sounds like a drug, but what would Veronica have to do with it? This makes no sense. Knowing he was going to die, why would Perry write this message and go to such elaborate measures to get it to me? Was this his final game?

He certainly knew that Veronica is my Achilles Heel. Is this his last-ditch bid for control by getting under my skin and making me spin my wheels endlessly?

The skin on the back of my neck prickles. That same feeling of being watched descends over me. It presses down on me like a stone. I look up and stare through the windshield. I see two men, one in a charcoal gray suit and the other in a dark blue suit, standing with a corrections officer. Judging by the way the sun glints off a few stars on the man's collar, I'd say he's probably a pretty high ranking CO. All three are staring straight at me.

A dark, ominous feeling envelops me as I stare back at them. It could be a coincidence. Just a matter of happenstance that they're standing at the gate, speaking with some anonymous high-ranking CO, staring at me like they want to kill me. It's possible it's nothing. Maybe I'm letting the paranoia of the guard inside bleed over into the day beyond the walls.

But everything inside of me is ringing wildly. Every warning bell and red flag is going off, urging me to get out of here. And if there's one thing I've learned in my life, it's to always trust my instincts.

I fold the letter and slip it back into my pocket, then start my car and pull out of the lot. I keep my eyes on the rearview mirror, looking for a tail, but don't see one.

"Doesn't mean they're not back there though," I mutter.

I drive on and think about Perry's note. Xytophyl. I have no idea what it is, nor what the connection to Veronica— or her death— might be, but I am going to find out. I have no idea where it will lead and given the fact that somebody was potentially able to get to a high-profile prisoner like Perry to silence him, it might be dangerous. But I need answers. I deserve answers. More than that though, Veronica deserves answers.

And so, I drive on.

THE END

Thank you!
I hope you enjoyed *I See You,* book one in Arrington Mystery Series.
My intention is to give you a thrilling adventure and an entertaining escape with each and every book.
However, I need your help to continue writing.

Being a new indie writer is tough.
I don't have a large budget, huge following, or any of the cutting edge marketing techniques.
So, all I kindly ask is that if you enjoyed this book, please take a moment of your time and leave me a review

and maybe recommend the book to a fellow book lover or two.

This way I can continue to write all day and night and bring you more books.

I cannot wait to share with you the upcoming sequel!

Your writer friend,
Elle Gray

CONNECT WITH ELLE GRAY

Loved the book? Don't miss out on future reads! Join my newsletter and receive updates on my latest releases, insider content, and exclusive promos. Plus, as a thank you for joining, you'll get a FREE copy of my book Deadly Pursuit!

Deadly Pursuit follows the story of Paxton Arrington, a police officer in Seattle who uncovers corruption within his own precinct. With his career and reputation on the line, he enlists the help of his FBI friend Blake Wilder to bring down the corrupt Strike Team. But the stakes are high, and Paxton must decide whether he's willing to risk everything to do the right thing.

Claiming your freebie is easy! Visit
https://dl.bookfunnel.com/513mluk159
and sign up with your email!

Want more ways to stay connected? Follow me on Facebook and Instagram or sign up for text notifications by texting "blake" to 844-552-1368. Thanks for your support and happy reading!

ALSO BY ELLE GRAY

Blake Wilder FBI Mystery Thrillers

Book One - The 7 She Saw
Book Two - A Perfect Wife
Book Three - Her Perfect Crime
Book Four - The Chosen Girls
Book Five - The Secret She Kept
Book Six - The Lost Girls
Book Seven - The Lost Sister
Book Eight - The Missing Woman
Book Nine - Night at the Asylum
Book Ten - A Time to Die
Book Eleven - The House on the Hill
Book Twelve - The Missing Girls
Book Thirteen - No More Lies
Book Fourteen - The Unlucky Girl
Book Fifteen - The Heist
Book Sixteen - The Hit List
Book Seventeen - The Missing Daughter
Book Eighteen - The Silent Threat
Book Nineteen - A Code to Kill
Book Twenty - Watching Her
Book Twenty-One - The Inmate's Secret
Book Twenty-Two - A Motive to Kill
Book Twenty-Three - The Kept Girls

A Pax Arrington Mystery
Free Prequel - Deadly Pursuit
Book One - I See You
Book Two - Her Last Call
Book Three - Woman In The Water
Book Four- A Wife's Secret

Storyville FBI Mystery Thrillers
Book One - The Chosen Girl
Book Two - The Murder in the Mist
Book Three - Whispers of the Dead
Book Four - Secrets of the Unseen
Book Five - The Way Back Home

A Sweetwater Falls Mystery
Book One - New Girl in the Falls
Book Two - Missing in the Falls
Book Three - The Girls in the Falls
Book Four - Memories of the Falls
Book Five - Shadows of the Falls
Book Six - The Lies in the Falls
Book Seven - Forbidden in the Falls
Book Eight - Silenced in the Falls

ALSO BY
ELLE GRAY | K.S. GRAY

Olivia Knight FBI Mystery Thrillers
Book One - New Girl in Town
Book Two - The Murders on Beacon Hill
Book Three - The Woman Behind the Door
Book Four - Love, Lies, and Suicide
Book Five - Murder on the Astoria
Book Six - The Locked Box
Book Seven - The Good Daughter
Book Eight - The Perfect Getaway
Book Nine - Behind Closed Doors
Book Ten - Fatal Games
Book Eleven - Into the Night
Book Twelve - The Housewife
Book Thirteen - Whispers at the Reunion

ALSO BY
ELLE GRAY | JAMES HOLT

The Florida Girl FBI Mystery Thrillers
Book One - The Florida Girl
Book Two - Resort to Kill
Book Three - The Runaway
Book Four - The Ransom
Book Five - The Unknown Woman

Made in the USA
Columbia, SC
01 July 2025